PAINE FOR THE HOLIDAYS

A STANDALONE HOLIDAY PARANORMAL ROMANCE

MONSTERS OF THE DIVIDE
BOOK 1

T. B. WIESE

OTHER BOOKS IN THIS WORLD

- Paine for the Holidays
- A Vexing Valentines (coming late March 2024)
- A Malicious Summer Vacation (coming summer 2024)
- Hunted on Halloween (coming Oct. 2024)

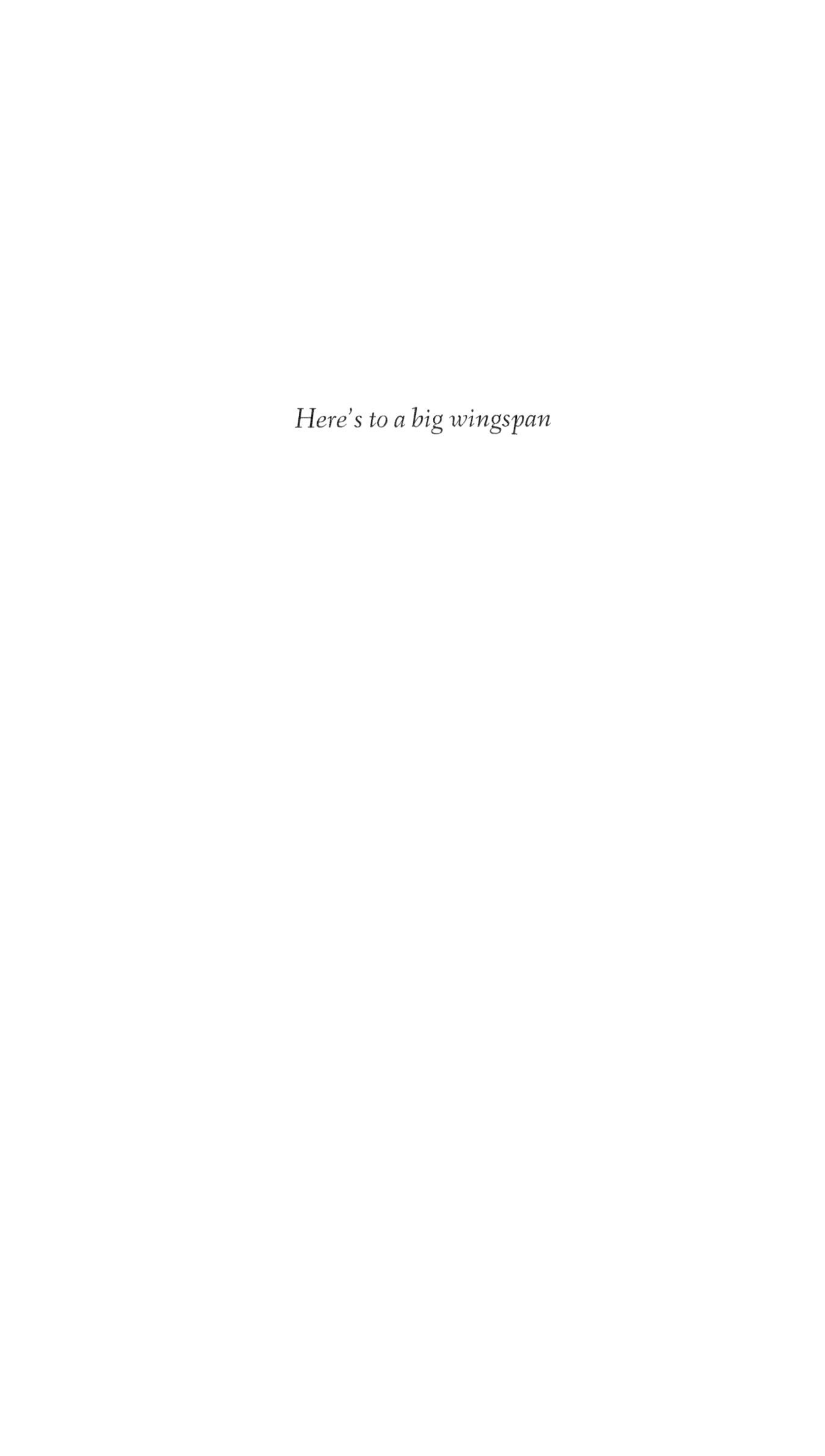

Here's to a big wingspan

AUTHOR'S NOTE

**Please take care of yourself and your mental health

Paine for the Holidays is an ADULT paranormal romance that contains elements such as: monsters, violence, swearing, mention of domestic abuse off page, blood, gore, Christmas and other religious holidays, and sexually explicit scenes ... with monsters.

MONSTERS OF THE DIVIDE

*Most of these are only briefly mentioned in passing, so don't feel too overwhelmed.

Dremar (Our MMC) - *Think vampire and gargoyle. This species has different colored skin. Our MMC has blue-grey skin that is smooth and hairless, but others have shades of red or green or black ... Eyes to match their skin color. Males and females have curly horns like an antelope. They are very fast on foot, even faster when flying. They have bat-like wings, a snake-like tail, fangs, and claws. They drink blood, not to survive, but to obtain power. They heal very quickly. Any being that they've tasted the blood of, they can incinerate with a thought. The dremar, but especially our MMC, are feared by other monsters.*

Xani - *Scaled skin that is very tough. Hairless. Usually green but can be other colors. They have reflective, reptile-like eyes. Sharp teeth. Extremely fast. Can walk upright or on all fours. They have snake-like tails, and hate the light, always sticking to shadows unless the hunt of a prey brings them out.*

Joteunn - *Fur-covered like a werewolf, only they don't shift. They have wolf-like ears and a snout with sharp teeth and fangs. They are pretty large comparatively in the monster world and are extremely strong. They heal very quickly as long as they have the magic to do so. They occasionally run in packs but prefer to hunt solo (as most monsters do). They do howl and bark to communicate, though they also speak.*

Grateslung - *Snake-like creature with the bottom half of a snake, the top half looks like a gargoyle without wings. Stone-like skin on the body, scaled skin on the lower half. Usually shades of grey or black but can be different colors. Their saliva is venomous, and they are very strong and fast.*

Quilen - *Tall, humanoid monster that's thin but muscled. They have branch-like horns that look too heavy to hold up. They are dark skinned with black eyes, long spindly fingers with claws. They aren't the fastest of monsters, but they are strong and can slip between shadows.*

Grae - *Feathered all over. Humanoid body with a sharp beak, eagle talons for feet, and wings for arms. They are not the smartest monster - they are more animalistic.*

Nepha - *Humanoid with metallic feathered wings. These are the creatures Angles were modeled from. They are exceptional hunters - even our MMC is wary of them. They are beautiful but cruel. Most believe that if they have hearts, they are made of stone.*

Hellhounds - *Large dog-like creatures the size of a pony. They do not speak. They hunt in packs, but once their prey is caught, it's every hellhound for themselves. They are a* little further down on the food chain in the monster realm, which is why they tend to stay in groups.

Anza - Smaller comparatively in the monster realm - about the size of the average human female. They have shimmery skin like starlight. They are pretty and disarming. They are one of the fastest monsters, able to move so quickly they are a blur. They have sharp teeth, a hypnotizing gaze, and can secrete hallucinogens from their skin to incapacitate their prey, which they like to peel and eat. Death by anza is very slow and painful. Not only can they heal themselves, but they can heal others - if you can convince them to.

Unicorns - They look just like our myths. Horse-like creatures with a single horn. But these unicorns are carnivorous with serrated teeth, razor sharp hooves, and are so strong, they can cave in a monster's chest with one kick. Their horns also emit a strong electric shock that can incapacitate or even kill.

We might meet more monsters in the upcoming books in this series, but these are all the ones in this story.
    Enjoy.

THE SIXTY SECONDS THAT CHANGED THE WORLD

Monsters are real.

Seventy-two years ago, they came.

Supposedly, at first, everyone thought it was a hoax. But it didn't take long for the world to realize that what was happening was indeed real. You can still find old clips of videos people took on their phones that night.

The monsters came through what we now call The Divide—the invisible barrier that separated our realm from theirs. Apparently, all throughout history, the occasional monster would get through—those folktales of werewolves, vampires, and fae started from somewhere. But that night, they all just ... appeared. So many humans lost their lives. The monsters took what they wanted ... blood, bones, fear, souls. Weapons didn't work on most of them ... with their tough skin, scales, super speed, wings, regenerative healing ... The humans were no match. It was a bloodbath. Then six hours after they appeared, they all just vanished.

The entire planet was still reeling by the attack when it happened the next night, and the next. Always at the same time. Always for six hours. It wasn't until almost a week of the occurrences that someone discovered that the first night the monsters came through, all time stood still for one full minute. Clocks ceased ticking, tides froze, the world stopped turning. No one noticed, because well, monsters. And no one really knows how life on earth survived the literal freezing of time. Time hasn't stopped again since that first night, but the monsters still come.

Humanity's saving grace came with the discovery of magic symbols with the power to keep the monsters out. Who discovered it? That truth is buried under wild conjectures, outlandish legends, and fantastical myths. So, who knows?

And here we are. Life goes on. We go about the monster-free hours almost as normally as before, as if we're trying to ignore the nightmare we know is coming with the fall of The Divide every day. But in the backs of our minds, we all know ...

The monsters *are* coming, and if you want to survive, there are only three rules:

Make sure the correct symbols are carved deep into your threshold and every windowsill.

Be sure you recharge the symbols with a few drops of your blood at least once a month to keep the monsters out.

And whatever you do, don't go outside after the final curfew siren.

CHAPTER 1

MIRA

I'm not going to make it.

Fuck. Fuck. Fuck. I'm going to die, and all for a little glass unicorn.

I'm sure my heart is going to give out at any moment. I hate cardio, but running, running is the absolute worst. Unless you need to run for your life.

Fuck.

With gasping breaths, I pump my arms, the small gift bag in my hand flapping and crinkling. The clip of my low-heeled boots rings out in the near silent streets. My chest burns, but I don't stop. My townhouse is still several blocks away. I know I'm not going to make it, but still, if it's a choice between death by heart attack or death by monster ... somehow, I get my legs to move faster.

The blare of the first curfew siren startles me, and I nearly fall on my face. My arms windmill wildly as I stumble, and the little bag in my hand goes flying, disappearing in a bush somewhere to my right.

Damn it. I manage to stay on my feet, glancing at the shrubs, indecision warring inside me. I should go get the bag. I should run. But ...

The only reason I was out this late was to get that stupid present for my younger sister. This is the first year she's coming to visit me after I moved away from the small town where we grew up ... the first time I've seen her in ...

Shame hangs heavily around my heart as I count back five years from my age. Thirty-three. My little sister turned thirty-three this year, and I missed it, and the last one, and the one before that. But she's coming tomorrow to see me for Christmas. And I'll be dead.

Just a few hours ago, we were laughing and chatting on the phone. We wished each other a happy Christmas eve, and before she hung up, she promised to go online and buy the ridiculously expensive train ticket. The thought of not having a gift for my sister on Christmas morning drove me out of my house. I knew exactly what I wanted to get her and figured it would be a quick trip. Again, I glance towards the bushes, not seeing where the bag holding the little glass unicorn landed.

When we were little, my sister used to press her face to the window during The Divide hours. Mom used to yell and try to drag her away, but she'd always go back, swearing that unicorns were real, and she was going to see one.

The second curfew alarm shrieks through the air. I jump as the automated voice announces, "One Minute until The Divide Breach."

A shiver of fear races down my spine, and I kick back into a sprint, leaving my sister's gift behind. I can't get enough air. I'm slowing down. My entire body hurts.

Maybe death by monster would be preferable to this damnable running. Well, it depends on the monster.

I shake my head. *Focus, Mira.*

Tears fill my eyes, and my throat burns. I'm not going to make it home. All for a silly glass-blown unicorn.

Sheer terror drives me on. I don't bother trying to call out for help. Everyone knows not to open their doors so close to curfew. And even if someone did, it wouldn't matter anyway. Only my blood protects me—my blood on the symbols carved into the thresholds of the doors and windowsills of my townhouse.

We've all hidden and cowered in our homes, covering our ears or turning up the tv against the screams of someone caught outside after The Divide goes down. And now, those screams are going to be mine.

Two blocks.

I'm not going to make it.

The final warning siren goes off, announcing my impending death. Terror seizes me, and my body threatens to freeze on the spot. But I keep running.

A roar screams through the night. The dark windows of the high-rise to my right actually vibrate with the sound. I can't see where I'm going through my tears. This is it. I'm going to die on Christmas eve.

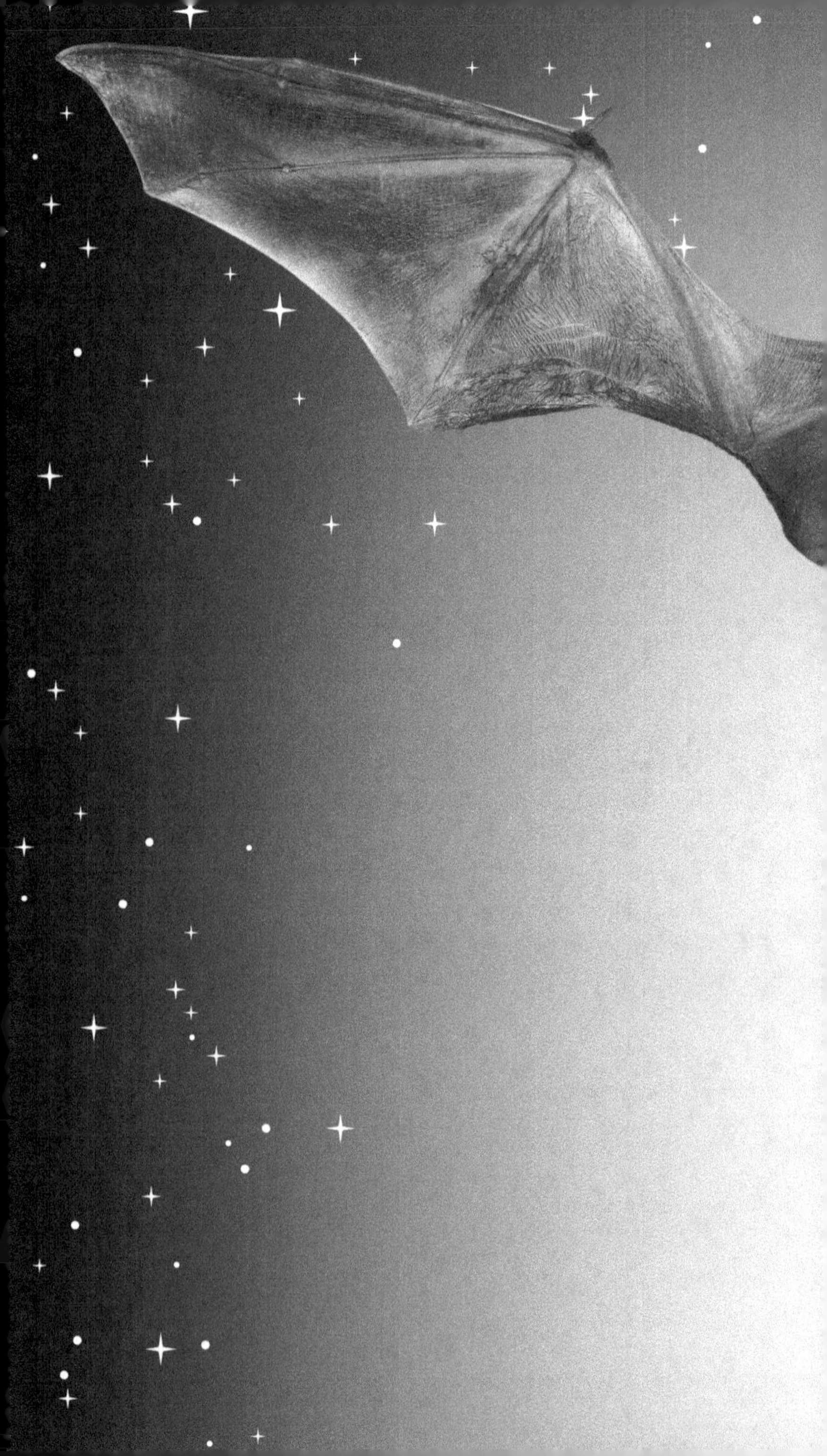

CHAPTER 2

PAINE

The Divide is about to come down. It's been a while since I've joined the others in the hunt. I haven't had the need or even the desire. Sure, when the wall between us and the humans first fell, it was exhilarating. The thrill of the chase, the taste of their fear, the scent of their terror. But after a while ... it grew tiresome.

But tonight, there's something in the air. There's a scent teasing the back of my throat. It's faint, coming and going before I can identify it. Cracking my neck, I slide my forked tongue between my lips, tasting the breeze. There it is again. Stronger. It's laced with fear, but I can still taste it, the wild scent like, like ... I narrow my eyes, peering into the perpetual night of our world. What is that smell?

The Divide is so thin now, the shrieking blare of the humans' warning siren pierces my ears. As soon as the ringing stops, my skin tingles with awareness. I hear crying. Someone is outside beyond their protective blood carvings. She's close and she's terrified. Delicious.

A wave of dizziness has me bracing my feet wider. I rub my temples, closing my eyes. A vision of a woman appears in my mind, and my body goes utterly still. It's so clear it's as if she's right before me. She's running, well struggling to run is more like it. Her wavy brown hair streams behind her in a ponytail, leaving her neck exposed. Her skin is flushed with exertion, and tears wet her face. For one long second, bright green eyes flash in my mind, and my cock goes hard.

The vision fades, and I snap my eyes open, letting loose a low growl of annoyance at my reaction. Surely I'm just excited about the hunt tonight. It has been a while. Yes, that must be it. But still ...

My wings snap out, sending a shockwave into the air that carries my roar for miles. The humans call us monsters, but there are monsters among the monsters, and I am one. I am Dramar, and my kind deal in blood.

The lick of the other monsters' magic scratching at my skin grows less intense as they back away, and I roll my shoulders, acknowledging their submission. I've claimed this lost little human woman as mine tonight. If another monster wants to go after her, they will have to challenge me—and there are few monsters who would dare.

Though, maybe the others have grown bolder as the humans have figured out how to hide themselves away? Will I have to fight for her? I shake my shoulders, my wings fluttering. It doesn't matter. I'll gladly destroy any monster who stands between this morsel and me. I grin, my fangs scraping my bottom lip as I imagine the tearing sounds of flesh and sinew as I rip my opponents apart before I savor the human's death.

Shifting on the balls of my feet, I run my tongue over

my lips. The human woman's scent is getting stronger with every racing beat of her heart. I can taste it, her despair. She knows she's going to die tonight, but still she runs. They all run.

The Divide falls, and I roar again, leaping into the air.

The lights illuminating the night of the human realm are harsh, and I blink against the offensive green hum of electricity. It's crude and inefficient. We use magic in our world, magic we'd never share with our prey.

The air current shifts as I take a sharp turn around a tall building, the metal and glass spearing into the sky. With one ear tuned to the panicked panting breaths of my human, I glance up the tall structure with a scowl. We did the humans a favor, culling their population. They build on top of each other because they run out of space and procreate like the nobbins of my world. You put two nobbins even remotely close to each other, and you'll have thirty more within the cycle. Pests. Just like the humans. Good for sport and food.

I tilt my wings, rounding another corner. My mouth waters as she comes into view. Just like the vision I had, her hair streams behind her, her loud breaths echoing against the buildings. I swoop down, circling her. She doesn't look up, and I doubt she even knows I'm here. My wings are silent, and her sobs are loud and beautiful. Her fear is exquisite. From the corner of my eye, I catch move-ment. A quilen stalks down a side street, its dark eyes on *my* prey. Its branch-like antlers scrape against the glass of a window, eliciting a squeak of fear from my human.

I growl, and the quilen pauses. It turns its all-black gaze up at me but doesn't retreat. So, I let loose a bark, the deep sound rattling the glass of the buildings around us. The quilen flinches but holds its ground for three long seconds before it slinks away into the shadows.

A gasp draws my attention to the mouthwatering human. She's made the mistake of looking up. Her brilliant green eyes go round, her tears shimmering. My tongue flicks out. Delectable. Tucking my wings, my blood races like it has never done before. I dive, and my claws sink through her clothing, into her shoulders. The coppery scent of her blood causes my mouth to flood with saliva. I wait for her beautiful scream, but it doesn't come. She just grunts as I shove her to the ground, more blood blooming as the exposed skin of her palms scrapes against the unforgiving pavement.

Oh, I'll get that glorious scream. Landing on top of her, my body erupts with electrifying awareness. She's so soft, and I'm so ... hard. I'm painfully hard. I should not have gone so long without a hunt, but I know what will ease this ache.

My fangs sink into her neck, and her scream fills the night with a beautiful melody of pain and terror. She thrashes under me. *Yes, fight little one. Send your delicious blood pumping through your body.* I latch on harder, ready to tear into her flesh, but then her blood hits my tongue.

Bliss. Sheer ecstasy. She is sweet and spicy and decadent and ... *shit.*

My head snaps back. Carefully, I pull my claws from her flesh, and a displeased rumble vibrates from my chest as I stare at the bloody puncture wounds in the woman's skin. Her back heaves with her struggling breaths, her scraped fingers digging into the pavement as she tries to crawl away. Her terror rolls off her, almost obscuring her natural scent, the smell that burrows deep, coating my nostrils and throat. But more than that, her blood, her taste, races through me, coating every surface, embedding into every cell of my body. Her blood calls to my soul, naming her as *mine.*

My mate.

She kicks out at me, her screams still ringing through the night, though her voice is going hoarse. I frown as I watch her struggle in terror. What have the fates done to me? A human woman is my mate? This frail human? I'm a monster. I can't …

My racing thoughts stall as I stare down at her. This cannot be. But the ache in my chest that's pulling my soul towards hers confirms it.

She's mine.

I run my tongue over my fangs, and the instinctual need to protect my mate screams through my nerve endings. But beyond that, I realize … I want her. She is a new type of prey, and she will not escape me.

A jolt of unease shudders through me. We exist on separate sides of The Divide … The Divide that is only open for six hours each human day.

Fuck.

She tries to get her feet under her, and when I reach for her to keep her from running off, she screams again. Foreign magic prickles at my skin as other monsters close in, drawn by her fear, her struggles, her screams, her blood. I have to make her stop, or this is going to get real messy.

CHAPTER 3

MIRA

I tell myself not to, but I keep looking back at the monster that is about to kill me. My racing heart is still struggling from my wild sprint through the streets. And now, with the terror of my looming death, adrenaline dulls the pain I know should be screaming through me right now. The monster's grey-blue skin makes him appear like a shadow, and I shiver at his sinister presence. His wings flick and flare in constant motion, and for some reason it makes me think of how I clasp my fingers and worry my thumbs against each other when I'm anxious.

I don't know why he didn't rip my throat out—it sure felt like that's what he was going to do. He's probably playing with his food. Whatever the reason, I'm not just going to sit here. My palms dig into the pavement as I scramble, trying to get to my feet. The monster reaches for me, and I scream. My throat is raw, but I can't help it. My body releases my fear-filled bellow from my lungs.

I pull myself forward, but I'm not quick enough. Of course I'm not. His clawed fingers grab the back of my neck, and I brace for death. I hope it's quick. I hope my sister forgives me. What was supposed to be a happy Christmas reunion will now be an agonized memory for her.

My parents will be sad of course, but I wonder how long it'll take before one of them tsks with a shake of their head, lamenting how many times they warned me against moving to the city. As if the monsters don't hunt in the country. They are everywhere. A hysterical laugh bubbles out of my throat. I can practically hear the 'I told you so.'

The world spins, and I screw my eyes shut. I try to curl into myself, my body automatically protecting my vital bits. My feet hit the ground, and hands grab my shoulders. I hiss in pain. Immediately, the touch moves away from my wounds and slides down to my elbows. A deep voice rumbles from mere inches in front of me.

"Open your eyes, human."

His voice is like molten metal—dangerously hot. I peek one eye open, then gasp, and both my eyes pop wide. Up close, the monster is overwhelming. He's so broad, he blocks out everything else. I bite my lip, my fingers curling into my palms as my gaze darts around, looking for that other monster I briefly glimpsed as I was running for my life. But the one with the scales and antlers is nowhere to be seen. It's just me and the tall, winged man before me. No, not a man, a monster. His hands are still on my arms, and when I move to try to take a step back, his grip tightens.

My body locks up with fear, and I flinch, waiting for the sharp pain of fangs or claws or ... His touch lightens but remains firm as he leans down. The moonlight glints along his curling horns, and I wonder if he's going to impale me on them.

His eyes meet mine, and my skin starts to tingle like cool water on a fresh sunburn. At first glance, his eyes look black, but when the light hits them, they're revealed to be a dark blue, the same blue as his horns that curl from his smooth head. My eyes travel over him, taking in the various shades of blue, from the blue-grey of his skin to the inky-blue of his wings, and the powder-blue of his claws. Claws that are still pressed against my skin, but not piercing.

I swallow, realizing I've been staring at this monster, and the fear comes barreling back. Trying to pull out of his grip, I whip my head around, looking for help even though I know there is none to be found. The monster once again holds me tighter, but his voice drops with what I can only describe as a purr as he says, "Calm yourself, human. You are bleeding, and your struggles will only make your injuries worse."

Out of nowhere, my mouth pops open, and I say, "I'm only bleeding because of you!" I don't demand that he let me go, because when has that ever worked? But I do shove him. He doesn't budge, and I'm left standing in the grip of a monster, my hands pressed to his chest ... his bare, muscled chest. All that blue-grey skin is firm and warm under my touch. The only clothing he's wearing is a pair of pants, leaving the rest of him on display. My brain wonders if he's cold while also appreciating his lack of coverings.

What the fuck, Mira. Get a grip. You're his dinner.

The monster opens his mouth, his dark blue lips parting, but he's cut off from whatever he was going to say as a chorus of howls comes from my left. My head swivels, but all I see is the empty street, the shadows holding more nightmares that haven't come out yet.

I yip in surprise as the monster pulls me against him, his wings flaring then curling around one side of my body. Is he ... shielding me? No. I've never heard of a monster protecting a human before. He must just be defending his meal.

His head tilts in the direction of where the howls came from, and he answers with a growl of his own. He asks, "Where do you live?"

At first, I think he's talking to the other monsters, but then he snaps his teeth. "Human, where do you live?" Dumbfounded, I just blink up at the underside of his chin. Keeping his eyes on the street, his voice rumbles with a commanding tone. "The hellhounds are coming. There's too many. Where are the blood carvings that will protect you?"

"What? Why? I'm not going to tell you that. I—"

My stomach drops to my toes as the monster launches into the air. I scream, and my eyes water with the freezing winter wind. Howls and growls erupt directly under us, and when I look down, gigantic dog-like monsters snap their jaws at us as they leap impossibly high into the air. I didn't even see them coming! My screams get louder as one nearly snags the toe of my boot. The monster holding me snaps his wings with strong flaps, bringing us higher and out of reach of the teeth and fangs below. He pulls me closer and presses his nose into my hair. Is he sniffing me?

I mean, I sometimes smell my food before eating it, but this is ridiculous. I try to lean away, but his arms are like steel bands. I'm not going anywhere, but my body is in flight mode. Struggling, I twist and turn, but that only results in him holding me closer. His breath fans over my cheek, warming my face as he says, "Cease your struggles. If you were to get free of me, the fall might kill you. And if that doesn't, the other monsters will."

Anger rushes through me, and before I can think better of it, I snap, "It's rude to play with your food. Just kill me, or eat me, or whatever it is you're going to do."

He inhales again, and there's something soft in his voice as he chuckles, "Oh, I have plans to eat you, little human." Why does my core clench at those rumbling words? "But first, you must tell me where you live."

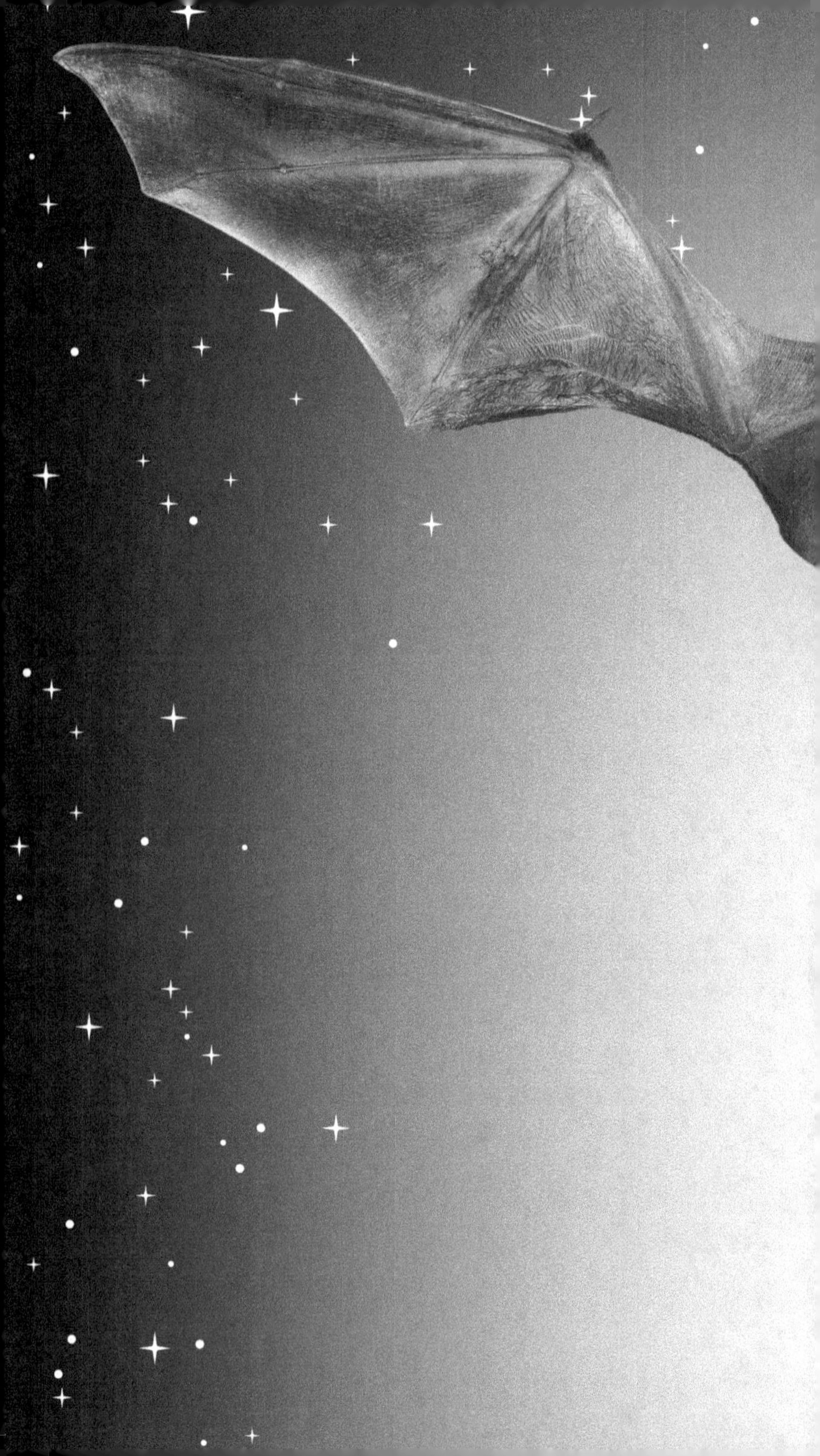

CHAPTER 4

PAINE

She is ... distracting. I didn't sense the hellhounds until they were practically right on top of us. I keep to the air, sending out pulses of magic to warn the other monsters away, but I feel some closing in. It's rare to find a human beyond their protective blood carvings these days. I'm not the only one who wants to play with the little human in my arms.

Well, they can't have her. She's mine.

But I need to get her to her home, to her protection. I am powerful, but I can only hold off so many monsters, and even less while trying to watch over her. My heart quickens with an odd emotion. Fear? I haven't felt it in so long, I'm not sure. I've tasted the savory flavors of fear countless times, but experiencing it is wildly different.

I realize I'm afraid of losing my mate. She's so fragile. The Divide has only just dropped, so there are still many hours for the others to hunt, to find me and the treasure in my arms. I must keep her safe until I can get her behind her blood carvings. And then ... I'm not sure. All I know is that she's mine.

I take us higher with strong beats of my wings, and she shivers. I tuck her into my chest, trying to convey with my touch that she doesn't need to fear me. Never me. But her teeth start clattering with her trembles. I have to shout over the rush of the air.

"You need to tell me where you live, human."

I don't dare go any higher, keeping out of the nepha hunting grounds, preferring not to anger the winged beasts. I angle us horizontally so my wings can catch and hold a draft. Gravity pulls at my human, and she instinctively wraps her arms around me. Yes, I like this. An involuntary purr vibrates in my chest, but she whimpers, probably assuming the sound is one of hunger. And I do hunger for her, but not in the way she fears. Her legs hang awkwardly, arching her back. While I'm quite enjoying having her softness pressed against me, she keeps trying to curl her knees into her chest. She'd be much more comfortable if she wrapped her legs around my waist. With a little sigh, I curl my thick, snake-like tail around her thighs, securing her more firmly against me. While she doesn't exactly relax, she stops her struggles.

She says something, but it's muffled against my chest. Her warm breath spreads heat across my entire body, pooling between my thighs. I shift, dipping my head so I can hear her, and I catch her stuttered chanting. "F-fuck. I d-don't want t-to die. I don't want t-t-to die. F-fuck. Fuck."

A nepha screeches, and I pump my wings faster.

The woman in my arms tries to swivel her head to see the source of the hair-raising shriek, but I'm blocking her view of the monster dipping in and out of the fast-moving clouds high above us. I must get my human to safety. Out in the open, with her in my arms and as exposed as we are, I can't possibly fight off the nepha without some harm coming to my mate. I need to get her away from here and somewhere I can try to wrap my mind around our situation. The fates landed me in this predicament, so the least they could do is give me a godsdamned minute to think.

My teeth grind almost painfully. A human mate.

I shake my head, focusing. Tightening the coil of my tail and one hand around her back, my other hand pats down her body.

Her voice squeaks adorably. "What? Stop. Hey!"

I slip the little device out of her back pocket, thankful for her tight pants for more than one reason ... they securely held her phone even through all her struggles, plus they hug her like a second skin. Doing my best to ignore the distraction of her perfect ass, I hold up the device, flipping it open. With a simple touch of my magic, the phone unlocks, and I search for the information I need.

She goes to grab the phone from me, but then realizes to do so, she must let go of me. With another squeak of fear, she wraps her arms back around my neck, and I nearly fall from the sky at the tight press of her body against mine. She feels so good here, in my arms. Too good. I need to concentrate.

Ah, there it is. Mira. Her name is Mira. And there's her address. I tap it, and a map comes up, showing me the way. Slipping the little device back into her pocket, I take the opportunity to feel her, to memorize her curves. I allow myself the luxury of letting my palm flex around her ass, and I ache to explore more of her. Some of her hair has fallen loose out of her tie, and it tickles my face. Pressing my lips to the shell of her ear, I speak loud enough to be heard over the whipping wind. "Hold on, little joy."

She tilts her head back to look at me, and I'm enraptured at her beauty under the moonlight. But I'm confused by the signals I'm reading from her body. She's shaking, her muscles tense. But the scent of her fear is much fainter than it was before. So why do her teeth rattle, and why are her lips tinted a pretty blue, almost matching mine? I don't remember humans being able to turn colors.

I keep the flap of my wings steady while I keep my gaze on hers. I purr softly, hoping to ease whatever emotions are causing her trembling. She stares at me, and I let myself get lost in her green eyes before she turns her head. A little gasp comes from her parted lips, and I find myself leaning in to kiss her cheek, but her eyes go wide as she says, "That's my house!"

I smile, pleased the deep smoky-blue color of her home matches the color of my horns. I circle above the row of houses all stuck to each other, using my sharp eyes and keen senses to locate any monsters that might be nearby. There are a few that are too close for my liking, so I send out another pulse of magic, warning them away. Mira shivers harder, and I frown down at her. "You do not smell this terrified. Why do you tremble so?"

"What?"

"Why are you shaking so violently? And you're turning strange colors. Why?"

I'm shocked by the happy sound that comes from her lips. Laughing. She's laughing. Her eyes sparkle, and her face lights up. She shakes her head as she says, "I'm f-freezing. It's supposed to s-snow tonight, and I'm n-not dressed properly." Her smile fades, and I wonder what I can do to bring it back as she whispers, "I c-certainly wasn't planning on being out this late."

I slowly begin to descend, and as I do, I wrap a hand around the back of her neck. "I'm sorry. I forgot humans can't regulate their temperature like I can." Shame spears through me—another emotion I haven't felt in ages. I'm not doing a very good job with my mate. I will do better. Rubbing one hand up and down her back, I try to warm her as I say, "I won't hurt you, little joy. You're safe with me."

My bare feet hit the top step in front of her door, but I don't lower her out of my arms. Everything in me screams that this is where she belongs—here, with me, where I can touch her, hold her. I can't let her go.

Mira's voice draws me out of my thoughts. "Are you ... are you going to let me go?"

My body moves before I give it the command, the instinctual pull of the mate connection kicking in. My lips brush against her temple, and I breathe her in. She's so still in my arms. Prey waiting for the predator to strike. Her blood calls to my blood. My cock presses painfully against my pants, the only clothing I'm wearing, and I curse the fabric keeping me from my mate.

But that's not all that's keeping me from her. I'm a monster, and The Divide will pull me from her in a few hours.

There must be a way. The fates wouldn't give me a mate so fragile only to rip me away from her. I'll figure something out, but first, I must make sure she's safe. Gently, I trace my clawed finger down her cheek, reluctantly lowering her until her feet touch the ground. I keep my eyes on her, because there's nowhere else I want to look. My gaze lands on her neck ... on my mark. It takes a great effort to keep my possessive growl contained as I say, "Go inside, little joy."

She touches the bite with a wince, and when she pulls her hand away, blood stains her palm. I lick my lips to see if the taste of her still lingers. It does, and her flavor bursts over my tongue. I hate myself for having hurt her, but at the same time, I'm barely able to hold back a groan as my cock jerks in my pants.

Her blood is so delicious. What will her orgasm taste like?

Her gaze returns to mine. With wide eyes, she stares at me, and my skin tingles with her attention focused on me. I search her face for any clue to her thoughts. I'm well aware that humans don't have mates. They speak of it as love—such a weak word for what my mate and I will share. The humans do speak of soul mates, but very few actually believe in the concept. They write of it in their books, thinking such a fated coupling is only a thing of fiction. But with every beat of my heart, my blood sings for her. How do I tell this fragile little thing that we are bound together?

My body tenses and my tail thrashes as my skin tingles with awareness.

Other monsters. They're hungry, and they're coming.

CHAPTER 5

MIRA

My brain is screaming for me to get inside, to get on the safe side of my threshold. But I'm frozen.

The monster in front of me snaps out an arm, and I flinch. Closing my eyes, I wait for the killing blow. My door crashes open behind me, the wood splintering loudly. My head whips around. There were four locks on that door. My attention snaps back forward as monsters snarl and race towards my townhouse ... towards him.

He doesn't turn at the terrifying threats closing in behind him. Instead, he keeps his dark blue gaze on me. He moves so fast I don't see it as his palm lands on the center of my chest, shoving me backwards. I'm weightless as I fly over my threshold. I land hard, my back slamming into the worn wood floor of my hallway. My head snaps backwards. Pain shoots through my skull, and stars burst across my vision. Snarls and growls come from outside.

There's a yip of pain, then a bellow of rage. What's going on? Is he okay?

Wait. Why am I worried about a monster?

I'm alive ... because he saved me. He brought me home. Sure, he sunk his claws into my shoulders and his fangs into my neck, but still.

Rolling onto my side, I get to my hands and knees. I sway, almost throwing up, but manage to keep it down. I crawl closer to my front door—my broken front door that's hanging wide open. But my blood carvings will protect me. They will keep the monsters out.

I'm dizzy and in pain, but through the nausea, my breath hitches at the scene out on the street. My monster fights with the grace of a dancer. He moves so quickly, he's almost a blur. It might be the concussion, but it almost looks like his wings glow under the light of the moon as he maneuvers around the pack of monsters. His claws seem longer than they were when he held me, as he swipes at a spider-like creature. It mewls, jumping away as it spits green liquid at him. He easily dodges, then spins on another monster, this one very similar to him, though its skin, wings, and horns are various shades of red. The red monster's snake-like tail whips out, slicing into my monster's chest. Blue blood wells up and spills down his muscled torso, but there's no wince of pain. No. My monster laughs, the sound sending a flurry of fear and ... something else through my stomach.

A pair of creatures stalk towards the fight. What did he call them? Hellhounds. The wolf-like creatures growl as they leap, swipe, and snap. My monster rips the head off a hellhound just as a monster with bones on the outside of its body moves with incredible speed, joining the fray. It's so violent, blood and gore everywhere, but I find myself moving even closer to the edge of my threshold.

My monster shouts at the red one. "You dare challenge me even knowing I own your blood?"

He what? My hand flies to my neck, pressing to the slightly swollen puncture marks. *He owns the monster's blood? Does he own mine? What does that mean?*

My question is answered as the red monster charges, his face pulled back in a snarl, his fiery eyes landing on me. He licks his lips as he says, "I want it. It smells good."

My monster roars. He doesn't even touch the red one, but its mouth opens with a scream. Fire spills out between its lips. A second later, its entire body erupts in flames. Its piercing cries fill the night, and all the other monsters scatter with fearful looks over their shoulders.

My vision tunnels, and I topple to my side. I want to close my heavy eyes, but my monster turns, and I'm captured by his gaze. He looks at me like he'd burn the world for me. Again, I blame my concussed brain, but I like that look from him. He strides towards me, seemingly unconcerned with his wounds. There's the slash from the red monster's tail, what looks like claw marks on one arm, and a bite on his side. I gape as his injuries begin to heal. By the time he reaches the top step and stands before me, his skin is unmarked. The only evidence of his fight is the midnight-blue stains of his dried blood.

He looks down at me with a frown, and I manage to sit up, pressing my back against the wall. Crouching, he reaches out, but stops just before his fingers touch the barrier of my blood carvings. He makes a fist as he says, "You are hurt."

My brain reminds me, *this monster tasted your blood.*

My body jerks away from him, causing me to wince. *Nope. Slower movements, Mira.* I go still, breathing deep, trying to keep myself from vomiting as he whispers, "Little joy, how can I help?"

When he moves even closer, I flinch again, trying to pull myself along the wall, but my body won't cooperate. The monster at my door crosses his arms over his knees. "Joy."

Further proof that my brain isn't working right, I ask, "Why do you keep calling me that?"

His head tilts. "That's your name."

"No, it's not."

"I saw it on your device. Your name is Mira." Fuck. He knows my name on top of knowing where I live. He must see the fear on my face because he curls into himself, trying and failing to make himself look smaller. "In my language, Mira means joy."

My hand lands on my neck again. It's no longer bleeding, but the twinge of pain reminds me how close I came to death. His eyes track my movement, and his frown deepens, pulling at his brows and lips as he says, "I am not Fae. I hold no power over your name."

No, he holds power over blood. And he's tasted mine.

He goes on. "To prove it to you, I will give you mine." He presses his large palm to his chest. "I am Paine."

My fingers tighten around the bite mark, and he sighs. "It's spelled PAINE, but I'm eternally sorry, little joy. It agonizes me that I caused you pain ... again."

My vision blurs, and for a moment there are two of him. I blink a few times, and when things clear up, I lick my lips. His heated eyes track the movement, causing my core to clench.

I do my best to ignore my reaction as I wonder what I should do now. Do I thank him for not killing me? For protecting me, and for bringing me home? Saying it like that in my head, I realize, yeah, I should probably thank him.

A monster barrels into Paine, hitting him in the side. I swear I hear bones crack as they tumble out of view. Before I can scramble up to see where they went, another monster slams against the invisible barrier at my door. I scream, falling backwards as the monster claws at the air, trying to break through. Its snake-like lower half coils up so it towers higher than my door frame. It hunches, slamming its hands against the barrier, its fangs dripping with what I can only assume is venom. The skin of his neck hoods out, and the monster spits. The poison splatters against the barrier and slides down to the stoop, hissing and bubbling the whole way.

Another winged monster, this one with feathers that look like they're made from metal, drops out of the sky. It grabs the snake creature by the tail and tries to pull it away from my stoop. Pulses of pain spear through my already aching head as the winged one screeches, "I want it! I'm hungry, and its soul will feed my magic. Its blood smells good."

The snake creature turns to fight the feathered monster, and with their attention diverted, I frantically look up and down the street. Where is Paine? Is he okay? A little voice in my head tells me I shouldn't care. He's a monster.

I'm sweating, and my arms are trembling. I've never passed out before, but I think I'm about to. Still, I strain to try to find *my* monster.

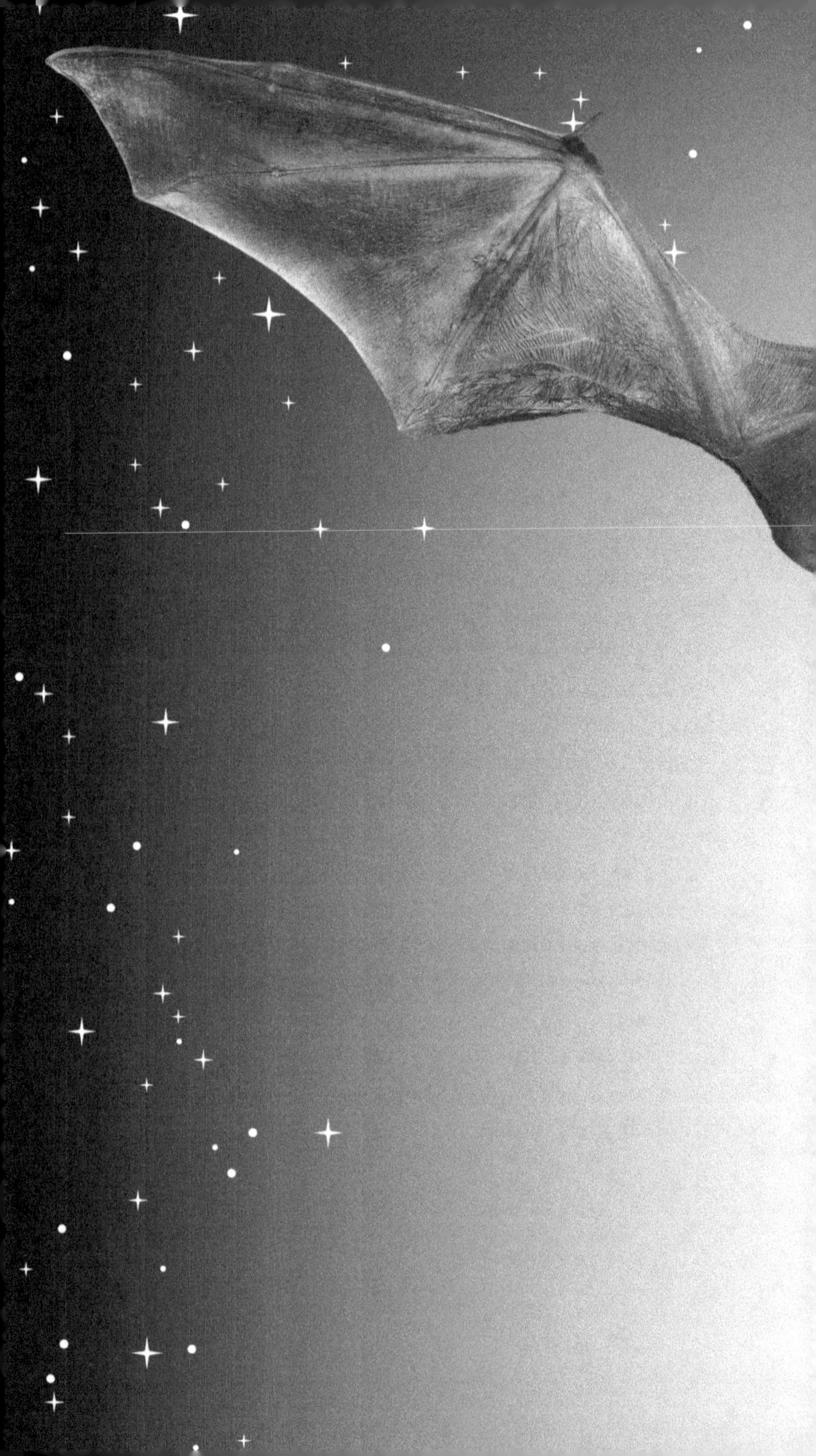

CHAPTER 6

PAINE

I'm thankful I got Mira behind her blood carvings when I did. Monsters race towards her house from every direction. It must be the scent of her blood. Even if it's only half as enticing to them as it is to me, I can understand their eagerness. And under different circumstances, I'd revel in this fight.

But she is mine, and though I know her carvings will keep them out, my entire body screams to protect her, to kill all those who are trying to take her from me. I won't leave her until The Divide closes and forces us apart. Speaking of which, my time is limited, and I don't want to waste it fighting these fools. Lightning quick, I snatch the snarling xani to my right, dragging into the air with me. With a simple flex of my muscles, I rip one of its arms off before tearing its throat out with my teeth. I toss it aside, ignoring the spray of light-green blood that splatters across my skin. My power hums in recognition as a joteunn charges in its blind bloodlust. Its wide mouth opens to reveal its rows of sharp teeth, the fur covering its body standing on end. I don't give it a second glance as my magic arcs to the creature and ignites the blood that I tasted several decades ago.

As the joteunn goes up in flames, its body bubbling and melting, the snake-like grateslung and feathered grae claw and tear at each other. Between blows, they cast hungry gazes towards my mate, fueling my rage. With a flap of my wings, I dodge a hellhound, only to catch the claws of a second one. Before it can leap away, I grab a fistful of fur, tug it to me, and snap its spine.

My attention is pulled back to the broken door of Mira's home. The grateslung has slain the grae and is now spitting venom and tearing at the blood-carving barrier.

Enough.

I throw my head back and roar. The other monsters freeze, and the grateslung looks at me, poisoned saliva dripping down its chin. I lower myself to the ground and stalk towards Mira's house. The haze of bloodlust fades from grateslung's eyes, and it bows and backs away. My intention is to ignore it as long as it leaves, but then I see her.

My mate is slumped over in her front hallway, her eyes closed, her breathing erratic. I pushed her too hard in my panic to get her across her threshold. I've never hated my name, but I do now. I am Paine. I am her pain, and that guts me. I roar again, and the grateslung isn't fast enough. With a snap of my wings, I'm on it, my fangs sinking deep. As soon as its blood hits my throat, I send my magic into the monster, setting its blood on fire.

I leave it in the street, its screeches fading as I stalk back to my joy, my Mira. She moans, but her beautiful eyes remain closed as she whispers something unintelligible.

Fuck.

The violence I just displayed wasn't enough. Spinning, I release a powerful pulse of magic that nearly drains me, but I don't care as I roar into the night. Silence is the only response, and I know my message has been made clear. Come near me or my mate, and you die.

Slowly, I turn back around. My shoulders slump. Mira is still unconscious. This can't be good. Humans are so ... breakable. What if I've broken mine? She's still breathing though, so that's good. Unfortunately, I'm sure no human doctor will come out during The Divide hours. I could hunt down an anza. They have some healing abilities, but I don't have time to find one, capture it, and bring it back before The Divide goes back up. And besides, I wouldn't be able to get an anza to her as long as she's within her home.

Fuck.

Hours pass as I stand guard, and I eventually feel the pull of The Divide. My eyes rove over Mira, trying to memorize every inch of her, watching her breaths, which have evened out a bit. Like a caged animal, I pace the small stoop, my claws occasionally grazing the barrier. The burn of the blood magic is painful, but I ignore it. Paine is my name, and I'll endure it as punishment for hurting her.

The magic of The Divide pulls at me again, yanking at my skin like it will rip me apart if I resist. Has a monster ever resisted and won? Not that I've ever heard of, but I tighten my muscles, digging my claws into the wood of Mira's door frame. I grunt against the pull of the magic as my skin actually starts to tear. My blood drips onto the stoop and splatters against the invisible barrier. I gaze at my mate for a long, agonizing moment before I drop to my knees. Using my own blood, I scribble a few words on the ground. My finger leaves a smudge on the last letter as I'm dragged back to my realm.

Collapsing on the grass, my chest heaves as my body quickly heals now that I'm no longer resisting the magic of The Divide. I stare at the stars, my hand pressed over my heart. I've found her, my Mira.

Now, how do I keep her?

CHAPTER 7

MIRA

I'm alive.

The sun slants through my kitchen window as I take another sip of water, and I roll my head from side-to-side. I slept through the all-clear siren—well, I guess I remained unconscious through the siren, only waking about two hours ago. It's well into the late afternoon now, and thanks to lots of aspirin, my screaming headache has lessened to a dull throb. But my shoulders still hurt like hell where Paine sunk his claws into me. Keeping my movements slow, I turn, reaching for the drawer in my kitchen that holds the rubbing alcohol and bandages. I shriek, jumping back as my butt starts buzzing.

With a little laugh, I reach for my phone. I guess I'm going to be pretty jumpy for a while. Sliding the little device out, I recall how Paine slipped his fingers into the back pocket of my tight jeans last night. A slow blush attempts to crawl over my cheeks, but then memories of the rest of the night flood back. The monsters. So many fighting right outside my door. The noise was deafening.

Clutching my phone, I walk down the long hallway. My door still hangs off its hinges, and I recall how Paine broke it down with a single blow. Pressing my free hand to the wall, I slowly lower myself to my knees, checking the carvings in the threshold. They're still deep and clearly legible. Just to be safe, I pull the collar of my shirt over my shoulder and press a hand to the puncture wounds. Collecting a little smear of my blood, I rub it into the stained carvings.

A click draws my attention, and I lean out, seeing my neighbor headed down her steps. As she turns to walk down the sidewalk, she sees me and stops, her eyes wide, her hand flying to her chest.

"Mira. You ... you're alive. With all that noise last night ..."

I sit back on my heels, waving at my busted door. "It seems I am."

Her eyes travel over my door, then flick to my bleeding shoulder. "Are you okay?"

Am I okay? I have no idea. But I nod with a small smile. "I'm fine, thanks."

She shifts in place, her gaze darting down the street. It's obvious she wants to leave, so I wave, getting to my feet. She waves back with a strained smile and hurries away.

I slap my hand to my door with a sigh. A project for today before my sister gets here.

Shit! My sister!

I hold up my phone, flipping the glass open to see a message notification from her. I press the button and hold it up to my ear as my sister's voice rings out. "Mira, please don't hate me. I was going to buy the ticket, I swear, but dad sprained his ankle, and mom has her Christmas party this afternoon, and you know dad when he's hurt or sick." I smile. Dad rarely gets sick, but when he does, it might as well be the end of the world. My sister's voice goes on with a plea. "Before I knew what was happening, I was promising mom to help around the house. I'm so sorry, Mira. I'll make it up to you. Love you. Call me."

I sigh before shooting her a quick text, telling her not to worry and that I love her too. Closing my phone, I slip it into my pocket. I feel guilty for feeling relieved, but I am. I'm glad I won't have to explain my battered body and my broken door. With my mind on the bandages in my kitchen, I begin to turn, but my eyes catch on something on my stoop.

Words scrawl there with messy blue smears, and as I lean down, I realize it's blood. Paine's blood?

I will return.

The 'n' trails off with a dark smudge. I swallow. Paine is coming back. Tonight?

Little butterflies flutter in my stomach as I recall how he fought all those monsters last night. I don't know how to describe it other than that he was violently beautiful.

Shaking off the memories, I clean and bandage myself up before fixing myself a snack. I stare at my reflection in the kitchen window. The bite mark isn't too bad—not as bad as it could have been, that's for sure. I didn't even bother to cover it after cleaning it. It's the claw marks on my shoulders that hurt like a sonofabitch. They're pretty deep, and I probably need stitches, but I just can't face the line of questions I'd receive at the clinic ... because yes, I was outside after curfew. It was my fault. I know better. And if I go to the clinic in this condition, they will call the police. I'll be stuck answering questions for hours. I mean, I understand. Those that live on the other side of The

Divide aren't the only monsters in the world. There are humans who hurt others and try to blame it on monster attacks. And while it would be fairly easy to prove I'm not a victim of domestic violence, I'd still have to endure the questions about why I was out, what happened, how I survived …

A long sigh deflates my chest. I'm not hurt that badly. I'll be fine.

A dribble of honey from the piece of toast I'm eating lands on my thumb, and I lick it away. It didn't snow last night, but it's still freezing. My sore muscles protest as I climb the stairs to my bedroom. I feel like I was hit by a car. Pulling on an old sweatshirt and my favorite pair of leggings, I brush my teeth and carefully run a brush through my hair. There's a large bump on the back of my head, but there's no dried blood, so that's good.

Once back downstairs, I haul my little toolbox out from under the sink and stare at my front door. A gust of winter wind whips my hair around my face, and I sigh. "Merry Christmas to me."

I make a quick run to the mega store and immediately regret coming out on Christmas afternoon. A man rushes by, pushing his cart with a wailing toddler in the little front seat. The man is not paying attention and nearly runs into a woman reaching for a pack of batteries. She hops out of the way, bumping into me. I grit my teeth, holding back a wince as my injuries and sore muscles protest at being jostled.

Quickly grabbing what I need, I toss my bags in the back seat of my car. Getting in, I stare at my steering wheel, hands gripping the leather. I wonder if my sister's gift is still in those bushes. I hit the button, and the engine rumbles to life. Heat from the vents blasts my face, drying my eyes, but I just stare at the parking lot.

Maybe that glass unicorn is still there.

I watch as a woman wrangles three kids into her SUV. Her shopping cart drifts away, and she throws her arms up in obvious frustration, her eyes rolling. Yelling over her shoulder for her kids to stay put, she chases the cart down, dragging it back instead of pushing it.

I should at least try to go find my sister's gift. I throw my car into drive, leaving the chaos of the store behind. My hands grip the steering wheel tighter and tighter as I get closer to where I think I lost the bag. Images of last night flash through my mind. Of Paine. Of the monsters. I force myself out of my car, and I shiver from more than the cold. Bare branches and prickly holly leaves scratch my hands as I search through the hedges. I'm pretty sure this is where I lost it. But I was in a panic. I try another cluster of shrubs with no luck. With a sigh, my arms hang heavy at my sides as I look around. Maybe I'm in the wrong place. Or maybe someone found it.

I burrow into my coat as a freezing gust of wind dances around me. I'm losing daylight. Resigned, I tell myself I'll go buy another unicorn later this week and mail it to my sister. I hurry home, and after two hours of grunting, swearing, sweating, and several tantrums, I get my door back up. Well, mostly. I think I'm going to have to hire someone to get it to sit all the way flush. But at least it's keeping most of the freezing air out.

Stashing my tools, I press the button to start the fire in my cozy living room and plug in the lights that I've strung up around my front windows. Happy peals of laughter sound from outside. I watch with a little smile as three kids run down the street; shiny new toys held aloft. There's excitement on their faces as they run around, playing with their Christmas presents.

I fall into my overstuffed chair, grabbing my book. I

snuggle under my favorite fuzzy blanket, curling my legs under me. Opening my book, I angle myself towards the fire. Several more hours pass, and when the first warning siren blares from outside, I realize I've only read two pages. I glance outside, noticing it's dark out. Am I ... am I waiting for him?

I pull my knees into my chest, hugging my shins. Will he really show up? And why? Surely, he knows I won't step foot outside my blood carvings. And he can't get in ... right? I grip my legs tighter, resisting the urge to add more of my blood to my threshold and every single window.

A hot shower. That will help.

And it does. As the spray falls down my back, it's like the water washes away my fears. The barrier will hold. The blood-carvings have always worked, and they won't fail now. Still, I jump at the second warning siren. Closing my eyes, Paine's blue gaze immediately pops into my mind. His smooth head with those curling horns and that pretty blue-grey skin. I was sure he was going to kill me. Rolling my shoulders, I recall the piercing pain of his claws sinking deep and the fear and agony caused by his bite.

So, what stopped him? After he bit me, he was almost ... gentle? Until he shoved me into my house. Granted, that shove saved my life ...

The final siren goes off, and I rinse the last of the soap from my skin. I turn the shower off, toweling myself dry. My reflection stares back at me through the slightly fogged-up mirror. I turn my head, looking at the bite mark.

A noise coming from downstairs makes me jump. I grip the towel tighter. How long was I spaced out? I hear it again. A knocking. It's past curfew, so the only ones out right now are ... monsters. But monsters don't knock.

Throwing on a fresh pair of thick leggings and a clean, oversized sweatshirt, I slowly make my way downstairs, my eyes pinned to the front door. The knock hasn't happened again, so maybe I imagined it?

I nearly stumble down the last stair as Paine's voice calls out softly, "Mira?"

He came back.

My slightly crooked door stares back at me as I wring my hands. I only hesitate for another moment before I reach for the handle. My newly blooded carvings give me the confidence to swing my door wide.

And there he stands. His dark wings are tucked tightly against his back, and his horns gleam in the moonlight as he smiles down at me. He's still shirtless, and every inch of his exposed skin is flawless, as if last night's fight never happened. My gaze travels down, and I get stuck at the obvious bulge in his pants. I struggle to swallow, wondering if that's all him or if in a cliche way, he has something in his pocket.

A deep chuckle snaps my eyes back to his face, and I know I'm blushing. His eyes sparkle, and I almost groan with embarrassment at being caught staring at his dick—his impressive dick, but still.

Thankfully, I'm saved from my mortification as he unwinds his arms from where he was holding them behind his back. He holds out two items. One is my little gift bag from last night. It's slightly crumpled, and there are mud stains on the little string handles. My eyes go wide as I reach for it. He found it. In all that chaos, he was paying attention. How ... sweet?

I wonder if the unicorn made it without breaking. Just before I reach the threshold, I stop and pull back. Paine's smile slips, but he's quick to put it back in place as he sets the bag on the ground. Standing back up, he holds out the other box. It's small and white with a glittery bow.

My gaze finds his again, and his smile widens. He's actually quite sexy when he smiles. Who am I kidding? He's also sexy when he's roaring to the skies and tearing monster's heads from their bodies.

Wait, what?

I look between the little box and Paine's eyes as he says, "Merry Christmas, little joy."

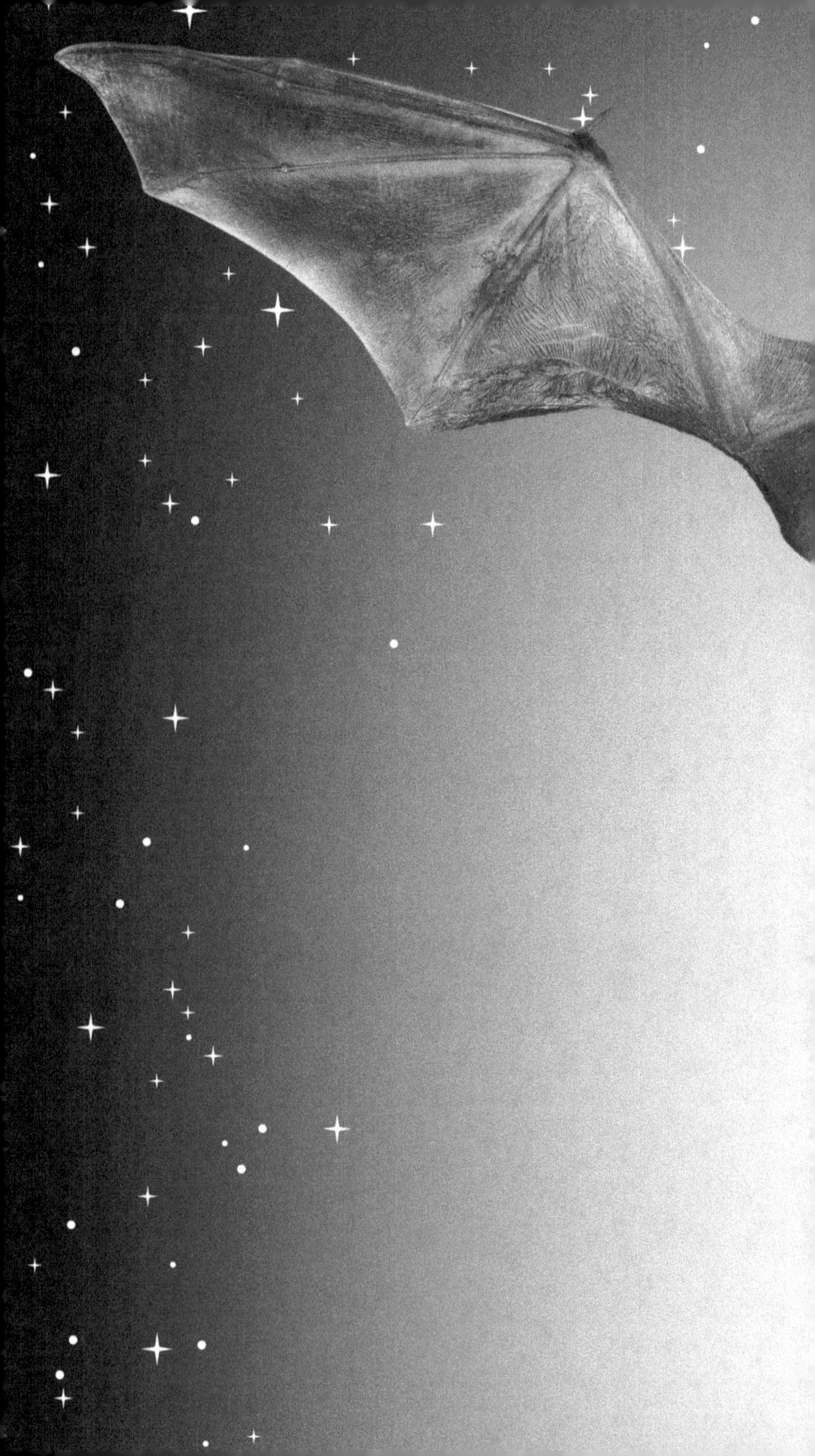

CHAPTER 8

PAINE

My little joy seems confused. Am I doing this Christmas thing wrong? I must have messed something up in my eagerness to please my mate. I spent the entire turn of the human day researching, then I hunted. Bright green eyes haunted me, making the turn the longest of my life. I'd never been more eager for The Divide to drop.

I don't really understand the human holidays. This one involves a magic baby, bringing trees inside, putting lights and decorations outside, and giving gifts. Or maybe she doesn't celebrate Christmas. Panic makes my palms sweat as I think through all the human traditions during this time of year. Does she celebrate Bodhi day, Hanukkah, Yule, Kwanzaa?

My hand starts to lower as yet another new emotion crashes into me ... uncertainty. This woman has me feeling lost, battered by darkness, unsure of which direction to go to reach the light.

Her voice pulls me from my thoughts. "Is ... is that really for me?"

And just like that, her words pull the smile back to my lips, and I nod. "I've never done human Christmas, well any human holidays for that matter." My brows furrow. "What's with the one with the bunny and eggs? Humans know rabbits don't lay eggs, right?"

Mira laughs, and the warm sound goes straight to my cock. Fuck, she's glorious when she makes that sound. I allow my gaze to travel down to where her bulky shirt hides her breasts. What might she look like coming around my hard length? What might she look like with her head thrown back as she rides me?

Thankfully yet regretfully, I'm pulled from my fantasies when she says, "Yes, we know they don't lay eggs." Her eyes fall to the little box in my hand, her fingers twined, her thumbs rubbing together. She doesn't want to cross her threshold. And while that stings, I can't blame my little human after what happened last night.

I crouch, setting the box next to the bag and slide both to the edge of her door. Standing, I nod to the gifts. I back up and take one step down, trying to give her space, but my body is reluctant to move any farther from her. My ears strain for any sounds of monsters encroaching on *my* territory—because this human is mine, and none shall threaten her.

Keeping her eyes on me, she kneels. I resist the urge to rub at the odd feeling in my chest when I notice her hands are shaking as she reaches for the little string handles of the bag. I stay still as her fingers cross the barrier and she snatches the bag, leaving the box behind. The strange feeling in my chest gets worse. I think I'm sad. I'm sad that she's afraid of me. Funny, I used to crave the fear of humans. The smell of their terror was like a live wire in my blood. But now ...

Reaching inside the bag, Mira pulls out the little glass figure. I know what it is because I peeked—a unicorn. As she turns it this way and that, the little string lights hanging in her front windows refract their light on the glass, making little rainbows shimmer on Mira's skin.

She's so beautiful.

A sigh puffs from her lips as she mumbles, "The tail is broken and the horn is chipped, but honestly, I'm amazed that it isn't in a million little pieces."

I cock my head down at her. "Is this unicorn important to you?"

She shrugs. "It's silly. A gift for my sister. She was supposed to visit me, so I went out, but ..."

Her eyes flash to my face, and her cheeks turn a pretty pink before she drops her gaze back to the glass unicorn. She stuffs it back in the bag, setting it on the floor behind her. Then her eyes land on the box still sitting on my side of her blood carvings. Slowly, she reaches for it, and I find myself rubbing my palms on my pants. Nerves flutter in my stomach. Will she like it?

Her fingers wrap around the box, and she holds it up, looking at the sparkly bow. She cocks her head, staring at it, her brows pinched. "Where did you ...?" I shift, shoving my hands in my pockets. My gaze slips to the right where the narrow alley holds the garbage bins for this row of housing. She must catch my glance because one of her brows raises. "You dumpster dived?"

There's a smile ticking her lips, and I shrug. "I certainly did not dive in. But no stores are open while The Divide is down, and even if they were ..." I wave a hand at myself. "I'm a monster, so ... Besides, there was plenty of discarded wrapping."

Her smile falls, and I internally berate myself. I should have just handed her the gift instead of wrapping it in garbage. Lifting my hands, I go to cross my arms, but then realize that might look threatening, so I drop them to my sides. But that feels awkward, so I stuff my hands back in my pockets. This is excruciating.

A softness falls over her face. "That's actually really sweet. I can't believe a monster brought me a Christmas gift."

I climb the step back to her stoop. Leaning a hip against the railing, I try my best to appear calm when all I want is for her to open my gift. I want to see if it will make her smile. I say, "Not just any monster, little joy. A powerful dremar. *Your* dremar."

Her gaze flies to mine. "What's a dremar?"

With a cocky grin on my face, I wave a hand down my body. "This."

Her head tilts. "I thought you were some kind of vampire."

My nose scrunches. "No, little joy. Vampires are parasites. Dremar are advanced beings with higher intelligence, and more power than a vampire could ever imagine." I shift, flaring one wing wide, and trace a finger over one of my horns. "And did you not notice these?"

She blushes as her gaze travels across the span of my large wing, then follows the path of my fingers down my horn. My dick tightens as I imagine her touching me, caressing my wings, grabbing my horns ...

I snap my wing behind my back and drop my hand. She blinks, looking away in what I assume is embarrassment as she says, "Well, you drink blood, so ..."

I can't stop the tsk that leaves my mouth. "We dremar don't drink blood to survive. I enjoy food as much as any other."

"Then why ...?"

"Why do you humans drink fine wine, or enjoy rich chocolate?"

Her eyes flick back to mine, her hand landing on her neck. "Blood tastes like that to you?"

Involuntarily, I lick my lips with my gaze on her hand where it covers the flesh that I tasted yesterday. I want more. Forcing my attention back to her face, I catch the flicker of concern in her eyes. "Yes, little joy. Now, open your present before your Christmas day is over."

She stands as her fingers pull at the bow, and it unravels, falling to the floor. As she lifts the lid, I hold my breath. Her brows furrow as she reaches inside and lifts out the shimmering strand. Holding it up, she stares at it as the rainbow of colors melt and dance with magic. She looks at me with a neutral expression, and my heart thuds into my stomach. She doesn't like it. I've failed my mate yet again.

"It's beautiful, but what is it?"

Hope tickles along my fingers as I smile. "It's a unicorn hair." I glance at the little bag on the floor before looking back at Mira. "I thought, with that glass unicorn, it must have been important, so, I, well ..."

She smiles, and the tension in my chest lessens. Then her eyes widen as she runs her free hand over the shimmering strand. "Really?" Her mouth drops open before her voice raises slightly. "Wait, really? This is real? No way! I didn't think they were real. My sister is going to lose her mind when I tell her."

A smirk pulls up the corner of my lips. "Best not tell her that unicorns are actually carnivorous, blood-thirsty beasts." Her eyes snap to my face, her mouth open in shock. I shrug. "They're quite nasty, actually. Their hooves are razor sharp, and they can crush a ribcage with a single kick. Their back teeth are serrated, and their horns can emit an electric shock that could even send me to my knees."

She blinks at me a few times before turning her gaze back to the shimmering hair in her hand. "Yeah, I think I'll keep that to myself." Her eyes find mine again, and there's a little smile behind them. "In fact, you could have kept that information from me as well."

I chuckle, and her smile grows. So beautiful.

I dare to hope as I hold out my hand. Her eyes land on my claws, and she swallows as I say, "If you wear it around your wrist, the magic will give you good luck." What I don't tell her is that it will also slow her aging process ... by a lot, as well as keep her from getting sick. I glance between the luminescent hair and her wrist. "I can ... if you'd allow me ... I promise you are safe with me, Mira."

Her eyes stay on my claws for another long moment before she looks up at me. She chews at her bottom lip, and I want to suck it into my mouth. I want to taste her. But I hold still, waiting. Will she trust me?

Slowly, she lifts her arm, and my heart stops. She takes one step but pauses. With a careful movement, I raise my hand a little higher, holding it palm up, and wait.

My mate's hand breaches the threshold, and she holds the unicorn hair out to me. I pinch it between my fingers, unable to look away from her as she lowers the back of her hand to my palm. As soon as her skin touches mine, my body melts and hardens all at once. Fire races through my veins, and my muscles flex with the desire to pull her to me and take her mouth with mine. But I keep my palm open and loose, accepting her trust as the present it is. Without breaking contact, I slowly push the sleeve of her sweatshirt up her forearm and wrap the unicorn hair around her wrist three times before tying it off. The glimmering strand looks beautiful against her skin, and she smiles down at my gift now gracing her arm. I did that. I put that smile on her face.

She pulls away, and while I lament the loss of her touch, I take comfort that she didn't jerk her hand away in fear this time. Holding up her arm, she turns her wrist, and the colors from the strand illuminate her eyes as she says, "Wow. I can't believe I'm wearing an actual unicorn hair." Her fingers trace over the strand as she whispers, "You didn't get hurt getting this for me, did you?"

My hands twitch with the desire to touch her. "No, my little joy. I am powerful enough that the unicorn I cornered submitted fairly quickly." What I don't tell her is that I syphoned magic from two monsters to replenish my power before I ventured into the forests where the unicorns roam. One of the two monsters still lives, its blood mine to command. The other I drained completely. It was a good meal of magic and blood, but there's still a hunger clawing at me.

A hunger I'm pretty sure only my mate can satiate.

She lets out a little sigh. In relief? I hope against hope that I'm reading her right, because I want my mate to care for me more than I want to take my next breath. Looking up at me, her eyes sparkle from the Christmas lights decorating the row of houses across the street.

"It's beautiful."

Pride swells within me. "You like it?"

When she looks back at me, there's what I hope is warmth in her eyes. "I do. Thank you, Paine. And not just for the gift. Thank you for saving me last night."

My body buzzes with pleasure. She said my name. But then the realization of the last part of her statement hits me. I surge forward, and she stumbles back. I regret my actions, but I need her to pay attention. Leaning my forearms on her door frame, I ignore the angry hum of magic as my nose nearly brushes the barrier.

I say, "You mustn't go out past the curfew again, Mira. If you want to leave your house at night, you will wait for me. I will take you wherever you please, but you must not venture out alone. Never alone."

Her wide eyes search my face as she nods. "I know not to leave my house. Last night was a fluke."

"One that almost cost you your life, little joy. I need your words of promise. I won't lose you."

Those last words just slip out, and I wish I could grab them and stuff them back into my mouth. It's too soon to reveal such truths to her. She won't understand. I can't spook her any more than I already have.

She tilts her head again, looking up at where I still loom in her doorway. "Before, you said you were my dremar. What did you mean?"

I swallow, my fingers clenching. How do I tell this little human that she is mine, my forever, my everything, mine to cherish, to protect? I'm a monster. Not just a monster, I'm a monster among monsters.

She misreads my silence and retreats another step, her hand pressing to her neck, to my bite mark. I almost reach for her, willing to endure the agony of the barrier in order to keep her from backing away. She wraps her other arm around her waist in a protective gesture as she says, "You were going to kill me. I know you were. But then you tasted my blood." I almost groan at the reminder of her sweet taste. "Does that mean you own me? Is that what you meant? Am I your blood slave or something? I saw you incinerate those other monsters. You can do that to me, can't you?" Her shoulder hits the wall as she stumbles, panic in her eyes as she backs farther away from me.

"Oh god. You can kill me with just a thought. Oh god. Oh god."

"Mira. Mira, look at me."

Her panicked gaze flicks to me, but she keeps retreating. Damn it. I press my hand to the barrier. My knees give out as pain rips down my spine. Not for the first time, I curse whoever gave the humans this knowledge—the knowledge to keep us out. Yet I'm eternally grateful that this barrier kept my mate safe last night.

Spasms cramp my back muscles, and I try to bite back my scream. Instead, it comes out as a growl which I'm sure does nothing to ease my little joy's fear. I choke out, "Mira. I won't hurt you. Never." I keep my hand on the barrier, willing her to believe me. "I would let the magic of this blood carving rip me apart before I ever harmed you."

Her eyes still hold some uncertainty, but she stops backing away. Relief punches through me when she actually takes a step towards me. "Paine, stop touching the barrier."

I shake my head, sweat flicking off my nose as the edges of my vision start to tunnel. "I deserve this and much more for causing you pain and for putting fear in your eyes, my little joy." Her form goes blurry as she runs back to the door, back to me. She drops to her knees, her fingers stopping just short of the threshold. My hand slides down the invisible barrier. I'm just a breath away from being able to touch her again. The agony steals my breath, but having her this close is worth every torturous moment. If I were any less of a monster, I would have passed out several moments ago from the prolonged contact with her blood-carvings. Pride swells in my chest. I am strong. I am powerful. For her.

"Please, you're hurting yourself, Paine. Stop."

"You care what happens to a monster, little joy?"

Her fingers twitch as if she wants to reach for me. "You ... you said you were *my* monster."

A lightness swirls around my heart, battling the pain. I feel my body falling, and there's nothing I can do to stop it as I collapse onto my side, my fingers still connected to the barrier. It's agony, and I want to pull away, but at this point I'm too weak. That's okay. I'm as close to my little joy as I can be at this moment. My wing bends uncomfortably under me, but I ignore it as I smile at my Mira.

"You know, your name doesn't only mean joy. It means delight. It means desire. It means pleasure. You are all that to me." I focus on her lovely face as the punishing magic starts to pull me under. "And I will be that for you, if you let me, Mira. I can be your pleasure."

The last thing I see is her bright green eyes sparkling with concern and ... heat. I've intrigued my little joy, making the pain worth it.

CHAPTER 9

MIRA

"Paine?"

His body twitches, his one free wing snapping taut before flapping over his body. Biting my lip, I reach out, unable to keep my fingers from trembling ... from fear, yes, but also in anticipation of touching him again. Before, when I ignored every rational warning blaring in my head and placed my hand in his, a tingling shock coursed through me. He was gentle as he wrapped the unicorn hair around my wrist, and I don't think I misread the yearning in his eyes. Now, as my fingers touch his hand, that same jolt of ... something tingles over my body. His grey-blue skin is smooth under my touch as I push his hand away from my threshold.

Paine's body stops twitching, and the muscles in his face relax. He really is quite beautiful, like grey-blue marble chiseled to perfection.

A growl sounds from the deep shadows of the narrow

alley between the townhouses across the street. The hairs on the back of my neck rise as another rumble joins the first, then another. Glowing yellow eyes blink at me and sweat breaks out on my forehead. Shit.

Will the monsters attack Paine in his weakened state? They're monsters. Of course they will. But if I pull him inside, will my blood carvings kill him? Death by monster or magic barrier? Is there a way to save him?

A wisp of shadow peels away from the sidewalk across the street. It slinks through the air, forming into a tall horned creature before dissolving into smoke, moving closer. It coalesces into what looks like a bull standing on two hooved feet. It growls, its luminous eyes on me as another monster creeps from around the corner. This one snarls, its body so thin, I can see the outline of its bones. It scrapes its metal-like claws on the street. Sparks fly up around it as it charges, barreling towards my house.

Shit!

My panicked mind blanks out, and I just react. Lunging across the threshold, I grab Paine's wrist and tug.

"Damn, you're heavy."

The shadow bull-monster slams into the thin one, earning it a slice from its claws. The two bellow as they clash. Blood flies as their terrifying growls and snarls fill the air. A screech from above draws my gaze, and my sweaty hand slips off Paine's wrist as what looks like a green dremar drops from the sky. If this is one of Paine's kind, will it help him?

The green monster stands on the sidewalk, its eyes flicking between Paine and me. It licks its lips and starts climbing the stairs, reaching for Paine. With a shout, I grip my monster and pull with all my strength. I topple backwards across my threshold, and Paine lands half on me, his bare feet still out on my stoop. His limbs convulse from the contact with my blood carvings, then his body is yanked away from me as the other dremar grabs Paine's ankle.

Digging my heels into the wood floor, I wrap both hands around Paine's arm. I'm in a tug-o-war with a monster ... and I'm losing. I can't let it pull me across with Paine. Shit. Shit. What do I do? I *should* just let go, but ...

The unicorn hair glitters up at me, and I grit my teeth. Reaching blindly into the gift bag to my left, I grab the glass figure and lunge forward. The chipped horn sinks into the green skin of the monster. It shrieks, I think more in surprise than pain, but at least it pulls back. With a grunting tug, I yank Paine the rest of the way into my front hallway.

Chest heaving, I flinch as the green dremar rams its shoulder into the barrier at my door. It winces from the contact with my blood-carvings, but then it speaks. Its voice is surprisingly light and feminine but with a bite to it. "Silly human. You take that dremar into your house? If you want death that badly, come out and I will grant you a swift and painless end." The glint in its eyes tells me my death would be anything but quick and painless. When I don't move, it snarls, clawing at the barrier before hissing and pulling back. "If you won't come out, at least give me the dremar. His power will fill me for scores of years, maybe even a century. You don't want to be around that one when he wakes."

I jolt in surprise when a low growl comes from Paine. His eyes are still closed, but a scowl pulls at his lips. Well, at least he survived crossing my barrier. The monster at my door flicks its gaze to Paine, and there's something close to fear in its eyes.

When I remain still and silent, it tsks, spinning and launching at the other monsters still fighting in the street.

I scramble forward and slam my door shut, which muffles the roars slightly, and I try to slow my breathing.

Looking down, I fully realize what I've done. Paine is in my house. Oh gods. What have I done? Maybe he'll remain unconscious until The Divide goes back up? What time is it?

I yelp as Paine stirs with a groan. Shit. Shit. Shit.

Backing down the hall, one hand pressed to the wall to help steady me, I keep an eye on Paine as his dark blue eyes blink open. He presses up to one muscled forearm, shaking his head. I take another step back, and his gaze snaps to me. I freeze like the prey I am, and his eyes narrow as he takes a deep inhale. His wings flare, scraping against the walls. A deafening roar sounds from outside, followed by a yip of pain, then a disgusting wet crunching sound. Paine's only reaction is a slight twitch of his wings.

The silence between us draws out. I refuse to move or speak. I don't think I can do either anyway. Paine remains propped on the floor as he slowly folds his wings against his back, the left one bent at a slightly odd angle. His eyes travel from my head to my toes and back up again. My body heats as his gaze devours me, and I fight the urge to squirm under his perusal. He takes another slow inhale, flashing his fangs.

Fear kicks at my heart, but my pulse throbs between my thighs. I didn't think I had a fear kink, and I certainly don't have a monster kink. Right? *Right?* I can't be having this reaction to the monster in my hall.

His tongue—his forked tongue—flicks out, caressing the tip of one of his fangs as he stares at me. His deep voice strokes all the inappropriate places inside me as he says, "Did you save me from the other monsters, my sweet desire?" That last word drips like lust and honey from his lips, and I press my hand harder into the wall to keep from swooning. Damn it. But then his eyes harden, and my fear ticks up to smother my arousal as he growls. "I was outside your barrier. You crossed your threshold to get me inside. You risked yourself for me, Mira."

I start to respond, but my throat is so dry. All that comes out is a weak croak, so I lick my lips. Wrong move. His gaze drops to my mouth, his eyes flashing black before returning to their deep blue. I swallow, managing to find my voice.

"The, um, the monsters. They were coming, and you were, well, um. It looked like they were going to hurt you. I didn't feel right just leaving you. You were unconscious and, um—"

I don't even have time to blink before he's right in front of me. My hair flies back with the wind created by Paine's lightning-fast move. It was a blur of motion, and I'm reminded just how far out of my depth I am. His breath puffs against my face, his chest pressed against my body as the tip of his claw barely touches the underside of my chin. The hall spins as my brain tries to process the emotions tumbling through me. Fear, arousal, confusion, anticipation ...

Leaning over me, his wings curl, not touching but capturing me completely. His other hand wraps around my waist, and my knees tremble as my back warms from his firm touch. His lips are a whisper from mine, and he holds my gaze, his eyes penetrating. A vibration comes from his chest as he says, "Never risk yourself again. Especially for me." The intensity in his gaze softens. "But thank you, Mira."

His lips brush mine. It's a feather light touch. Barely there. But it sends sparks shooting across my scalp, down my spine, into my fingers and toes, curling with delicious heat deep in my core.

I don't realize I've closed my eyes until I notice the warmth of him is gone. Blinking my eyes open, I stare at my empty hallway. The all-clear siren blares outside, and I sigh, running a hand through my hair.

Well, that was …

I bite my lip, my gaze on my door. Will he come back?

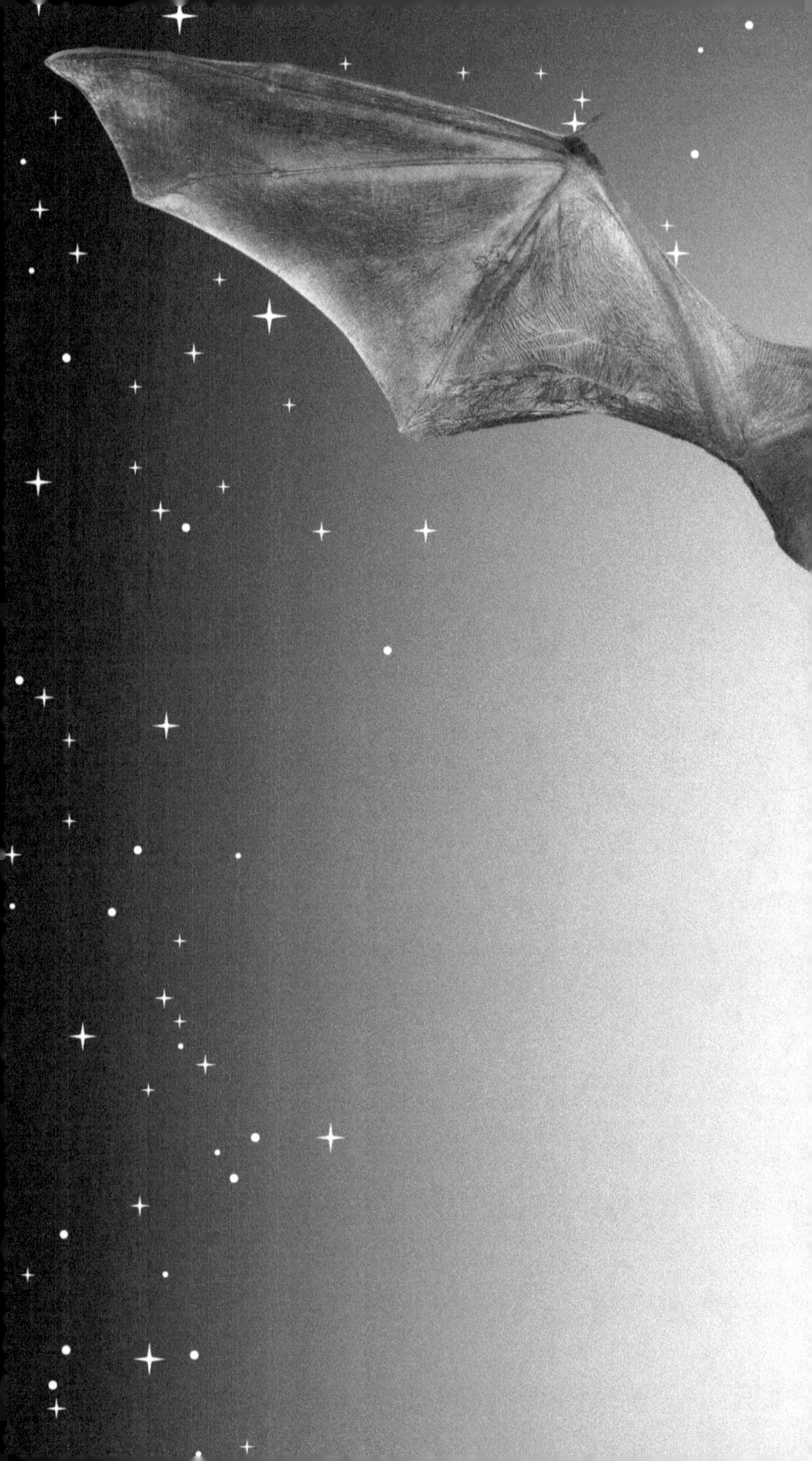

CHAPTER 10

PAINE

A grin pulls at my lips as I'm pulled back to my realm. My sweet desire is not unaffected by me. I palm my cock through my pants, the length throbbing with an ache to be inside my mate.

Rolling my shoulders, I flex my wings, testing the one I bruised when I landed on it. It's already almost completely healed. My grin grows wider, this time with wicked intent. I need to distract myself from the hours that I must wait before I can see my Mira again. With a leap, I go airborne, scenting the breeze for the dremar I smelled outside Mira's house tonight. I may have been unconscious, but my body knew my mate was in danger, and I heard its threats towards my mate.

When I finally find her, the green dremar has already scented me and is in retreat. Her wings flap with panicked effort as she tries to escape my wrath. Too late.

She is a young one, and I understand her motives. I was weakened outside Mira's door. If she were able to consume my blood, or worse, kill me, my magic would have become hers. It might have killed her, but maybe not. I myself took that same risk when I was a younger dremar, killing one much stronger than myself. I barely endured the agony as the foreign magic flooded my body. It was almost too powerful for me, but I survived, and now I am one of the strongest of my kind.

But despite my strength, I compromised myself and put my sweet desire in danger ... again. And to deepen my shame, *she* saved *me*. She is a worthy mate indeed, and I need to earn my place at her side. My fierce Mira.

I spear into the sky, darting high above the little green dremar. She looks frantically behind her, searching for me. She's so panicked, she doesn't think to look up. My claws grow longer, and my mouth waters with anticipation. Nothing will ever taste as good as my mate, but this death will be quite delicious.

I lick my lips, tasting the brief kiss I shared with her. Groaning, I adjust my cock before I tuck my wings and bullet from the sky. I slam so hard into the female dremar, she doesn't have the air in her lungs to scream. My claws sink deep, and my wings flare as I take us back up, high into the clouds. She finds her voice as I sink my teeth into her neck. Blood coats my throat as she screams, her own claws tearing at my flesh, but I ignore her struggles as I sink my teeth in deeper. Shaking my head, I rip her throat out. Her shrieks turn to wet gurgles as I go in for more. I bite and shred and rip. I tear handfuls of flesh from her body, then pull one of her wings off. Releasing her, I watch her body spin for long moments before she hits the ground with a loud thud.

I float in lazy circles above her, licking her blood from my fingers. Monsters start to circle her, snouts sniffing. Their eyes glance upward, waiting to see if I will leave her or set her aflame. I growl, building the sound into a roar that shakes the ground. I throw her wing away, doing one more pass over her twitching body before waving my hand in a gesture of permission.

The monsters pounce, finishing her off, some slinking away with an arm or some small piece of flesh. A few stay huddled over her, enjoying their meal, snapping at others who get too close.

Flying away, I head towards the storm clouds gathering far to the east. The rage of wind and thunder and lightning and lashing rain sounds perfect for my mood right now. Besides, I can't return to my mate covered in blood. Or can I? Should I show her what happens to those who threaten her? I keep my pace steady, thinking about my little human. I don't think she would receive the gift of her enemy's blood the way I would intend.

The smell of the rain and ozone reaches me, and I speed up. I hit the wall of the storm and I grin. Lightning cracks around me, and the thunder vibrates in my bones. I dance in the whipping winds, my pulse racing as I count the heartbeats until I can return to my mate.

Picking up in intensity, the storm moves away from my territory, so I leave it behind, flicking the rain from my wings. Dropping to the balcony of my home, I stride through the glass doors to my bedroom. I dry off and change into clean pants, remaining barefoot as always.

I'm painfully aware of The Divide, and every moment that passes, I feel it weakening. Clenching and unclenching my hands, I look myself over in the giant mirror hung on the black walls. My horns curl and twist into the air, showing off my age and my strength. My smooth head gleams, and my broad chest flexes with each breath. My claws are sharp, my fangs more so. Flicking it to the side, I snap my tail out before gliding against the polished wood floor, the planks so dark they're almost as black as the walls.

I am a strong and powerful male.

A frown pulls at my dark blue lips. Not just a male. A monster. Mira's fear may be waning ... slightly, but will she ever accept me fully? With a shake of my head, I scowl at myself. "It is early days, Paine. Give your sweet desire time. There were certainly flickers of heat and desire in her eyes."

My fingers trail over my lips as I once again recall that whisper of a kiss. My heart flutters. I want more. So much more. Rolling my shoulders, I stand taller. This is who I am. I am a proud dremar, and I will take the time to woo my mate. My eyes find the reflection of my bed in the mirror, and my blood races. Can humans cross to this side of The Divide? Could I have my little joy writhing in my sheets, infusing my home with her scent, with her cries of passion?

I pace my large room, the stars outside peeking between the fast-moving clouds. The life and blood of that female dremar has already recharged my magic, but I could go on another hunt and add to my power. Yet, to hunt means there is always the chance a stronger monster will challenge me. Lesser monsters could also try to gang up on me to take my blood, or even my life. If it were any other turn ... if Mira wasn't waiting for me on the other side, yes, I'd welcome a challenge. I'd hunt. I'd tear, and drink, and kill until I am sated and full of magic. That is the life of a monster—adding to and holding on to your power and magic at all costs. The strong survive and thrive. The weak do not.

Throwing open the balcony doors, I stride to the railing, gazing over the perpetual night of the monster realm. It's darkly beautiful. So very different from the human realm. There are no skyscrapers choking the skyline. There are no cars or buses or planes spewing toxins. And there's certainly no blazing sun whiting out the sky. Daytime, the humans call it. I've been to those human places where the sun shines during the hours when The Divide is down. At first, it was quite a marvel because it was so new, so different from anything I'd ever known. But the heat, the intense brightness, the feeling of being exposed ... No. I much prefer the dark.

I wonder which my little joy prefers, dark or light? She is a creature of both, and something in me whispers it would be wrong to make her choose.

I picture her here, on this side of The Divide, in this chaotic realm of midnight and blood and power. I've always loved it here, but now, I'm counting the moments until I can return to the human side of The Divide. The fates have certainly placed a worthy challenge before me, but what it comes down to is my mate's happiness.

That's all that matters.

My hands flex around the railing. Any minute now. I launch into the air with strong flaps of my wings as the Divide finally falls. It scrapes and pulls against my skin as I move from one realm to the next, but I welcome it, like nails across my body.

I smile as I come through right above Mira's house. Making one tight circle, I roar, reminding the monsters that this is my territory. Another larger circle confirms that the area is clear, so I dart down, enjoying the force of the wind pressing against my wings. I land on her stoop and run a hand over my horns. My stomach flutters as I reach out, but before my knuckles make contact, her door swings open.

There stands my mate with a ghost of a smile on her face as she looks up and says, "You came back."

CHAPTER 11

MIRA

I can't keep the smile from my face, and I admit to myself I was actually looking forward to The Divide falling tonight. As soon as the siren blared, my pulse kicked up in anticipation. And here he is. He came back.

I twine my fingers, rubbing my thumbs together as Paine stares down at me. His striking face breaks into a dazzling grin, and he bows slightly. "Of course I came back. You are now my only reason for returning to this realm, my sweet desire."

I feel my cheeks heating, so to try to distract him from my blush, I point at the stoop on his side of the door. He follows my gesture and kneels to pick up the velvet box. It's the same pretty shade as his skin, and I bite my lip as he gently cups the box in his large hand.

"What's this?"

I shrug. "Well, the tradition of Christmas is not just receiving gifts, but exchanging them, so ..."

His eyes go wide, and his gaze flicks between the box and my face. "You got me a present?"

My palms are sweating. "I mean, it's not a unicorn hair, or anything amazing like that. I just thought—"

He snaps the lid back, and his claws reach inside, carefully plucking up the silver charm. As he holds it up, the metal glints from the Christmas lights in my windows. It's a little dagger with a pair of spread bat wings. They reminded me of his … impressive wingspan. I resist fanning my shirt away from my chest as I recall how he encircled me last night.

His eyes settle on me, and I can't quite read his expression as he flares his wings slightly, saying, "They look like my wings."

I nod, lifting a heel and pivoting my toes into the floor. Paine's mouth opens, then closes. His lips fall open again, and it takes a long moment before he clears his throat and says, "No one has ever given me anything before." He drops to a knee, his sparkling midnight eyes looking up at me as if I hung the moon itself. "Thank you, Mira. I shall cherish it always."

I wave him off. "It's just a little gift. It's no big de—"

"Always, Mira."

"Oh. Okay."

He remains on his knee, his eyes back on the little charm as it dangles from his claws. I tug the sleeves of my sweatshirt over my hands, not sure if I should ask the question that's been burning in my mind all afternoon. His attention falls to my fingers curled in my sleeves, and he stands.

"I'm sorry, my little joy. You are cold. You do not have to remain here with me. Go inside. Warm yourself by your fire."

"You're leaving?" The fear I first felt for him has morphed into a fear of his absence.

He shakes his head. "No, Mira. I will stay. Your carvings are secure, but it gives me peace"—he presses his hand to his chest, the little charm clinking against one of his claws—"here to watch over you. I will make sure the others stay away. I understand this is the time when humans rest."

I'm not about to tell him I took a nap today so I would be wide awake in case he did come back. Instead, I shrug, saying, "I'm okay. I'm not tired or cold. I um, I wasn't sure if ... if well ..."

For a moment, I wonder with both a little fear and a concerning amount of anticipation if he'll be able to come across the barrier since I dragged him across it last night. But, when he takes a step closer, the blood-carvings hum in warning. Paine ignores it. "What is it, my sweet desire?"

My heart flutters at the endearment. I like it. I like it when he calls me his joy, his desire. It stirs me every time. I ... I like him. A monster. My monster. Waving at the threshold, I force the question out. "Could we ... talk for a while?" His eyes watch my face, and I know I'm blushing. "I'm ... well, I'm just so curious ... about your side of The Divide ... About you ..."

Slipping the charm into his pocket, he bows his head, then folds his body to sit on my stoop. He looks too large for the small space, and I bite my bottom lip as he shifts. Leaning back, he tries to adjust his wings to fall between the space separating the railing from the concrete, but there's not enough room. Shifting again, he turns his back on the street and lets his wings drape down the steps.

Slowly lowering myself to the floor, I can't keep my eyes from glancing nervously over his shoulder. He catches me looking and reaches out, stopping just before touching the barrier separating us.

"Do not worry, Mira. I'm paying attention. My senses are sharp, and my magic is strong. I will know if any others approach."

Pulling my knees up to my chest, I lean my back against the wall. "I guess I'll have to trust you on that."

He smiles. "You can always trust me, my little joy." With his legs crossed, he leans back, bracing his hands on the edge of the step behind him. "So, what would you like to know?"

A million questions tumble through my mind, but I can't seem to grasp a single one. Finally, after a long silence, I giggle softly. "Everything."

The skin of his high cheekbones turns a darker blue, and I wonder if he's blushing.

"Well, first, my little joy, you must know that I adore the sound of your laugh."

And now the heat that is staining my cheeks floods down my neck and across my chest. Who knew a monster could be so charming?

As The Divide hours tick on, Paine tells me of his realm. How there is no sun, just perpetual night. How power and magic rule there. How the weak are culled. It sounds brutal and violent, and something inside me aches for the monsters who spend their entire lives fighting for … everything. I'm surprised to learn they live in houses and have similar amenities to us, only they use magic instead of electricity. I admit to him that I always imagined monsters living wild in forests or caves or something. And to that, he just laughed, reassuring me that some do live in the wild, but most prefer the comforts of a proper home.

Our conversation flows easily, and I find myself

telling him about my parents and my sister who still live out in the country. When he asks why I moved away, I just shrug, telling him I wanted my own life, my own space. I feel him observing my face as I talk, as if he's trying to take in every nuance of who I am and what I'm sharing with him. He makes me feel seen.

When I ask about his family, he shifts, once again pressing his back to the railing. His legs are too long to stretch completely straight, so he props his feet against the opposite railing. The position looks uncomfortable for his wings, but he says nothing as he rests his hands on the concrete at his sides. He tells me that for most species, there is no family unit. Monsters are born or hatched and are often left to fend on their own before their first year has passed. Paine catches my frown and tries to reassure me by telling me that young monsters have strong survival instincts since they are an easy target. Most are born with leg and/or wing muscles already fairly developed so they can flee from the predators until they learn to fight.

He compares his realm to the animal kingdom here. The strong survive. The weak are food. That's just how it is.

When he falls silent, I do my best to swallow the ball of tears lodged in my throat as I imagine a little baby Paine having to flee for his life, his tiny wings pumping, his little heart racing. When a tear rolls down my cheek, Paine's brows pinch. He leans close, just shy of touching the barrier.

"Why do you cry, little joy?"

I brush my tears away, hiccupping through a smile. "It just seems so ... wasn't it hard ... when you were young? Weren't you terrified?"

His body rocks back. "You are crying for ... me?"

I shrug. "My parents always say my heart is too soft. I can't help it."

Leaning back in, his dark eyes travel over every plain of my face. "Do not waste another moment thinking about it. That's just the way of our world." His eyes darken. "And I think you are perfect, soft heart and all."

I laugh, deflecting his compliment. "Well, you've just met me. Give it time."

His brows furrow, and he reaches for me. His hand hits the barrier, forcing him to pull back, and he shakes his arm with a scowl. He doesn't reach for me again, but he says, "No. Time will not change my thoughts of you, unless it deepens my feelings."

Well, what do I say to that?

We settle into a comfortable silence, our hands close, the edges of our fingers just brushing the invisible boundary between us. I rest my head against the wall, turning to look at him. His position mirrors mine as we just stare at each other before he taps a claw on the stoop.

He says, "I must know, though I admit to holding this question back for fear of your answer." He pauses for only a moment before he goes on. "Do you have someone, Mira? Someone who holds your affections ... outside of your family?"

My heart skips. I always thought that expression was an exaggeration, but I just experienced it. I shake my head, and heat flickers in his eyes as I whisper, "No. I don't have anyone like that."

He nods, his gaze intense. "Good. That's good."

Slowly, knowing I'm crossing more than the actual line separating us, I crawl my fingers across my threshold. My pinky grazes the edge of his, and that simple, feather-light touch sears my skin. It flutters through my chest and curls my toes. At first, I think he didn't notice. But when I look closer, I realize his chest is still with his held breath. Cautiously, he wraps his pinky around mine, hooking our fingers together, and when I don't pull away, he exhales with a soft smile. Resting his head on the railing, he closes his eyes as he sighs.

We stay like that for a long while. No other monsters come near. The night is quiet and cold, but I'm comfortable sitting here with my monster.

My eyes slide open when I feel his finger flex around mine. Glancing at him, I see the small frown on his lips. His eyes are on our joined hands, and he hooks my pinky a little tighter as he says, "It's almost time."

I don't expect the hit of panic and sadness that slams into my chest as I look at the dark early-morning winter sky. How did six hours go by so quickly?

With a quick glance around, I slide more of my hand across the barrier, threading three of our fingers together. His warmth curls around my hand, and I find my throat tightening as I ask, "Will you come back?"

Shifting to his knees, he bows over his thighs, keeping all but my fingers on my side of the threshold as he lifts my hand. His lips press to my skin, and I shiver. If I were standing, my knees would have given out. His breath fans across my fingers as he says, "Yes, my sweet desire. The only thing that can keep me from you is your word to stay away. Until I hear that command from your lips, I will return."

Once again, I find myself at a loss for words. With his eyes on mine, The Divide goes back up, and Paine disappears. And for some reason, it feels as if my heart went with him.

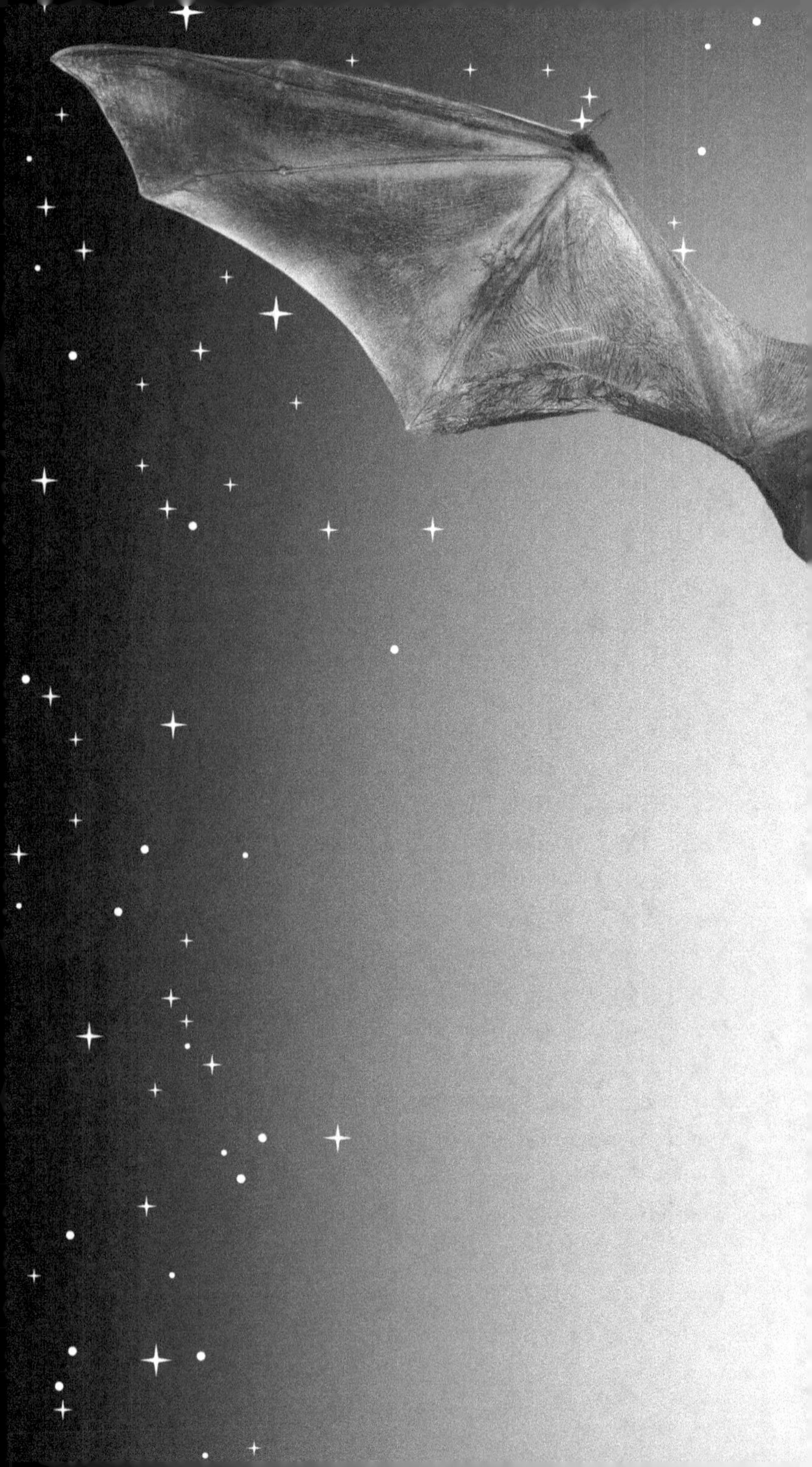

CHAPTER 12

PAINE

A full turn has almost gone by since I was forced to leave my Mira. My fingers ache for her touch as I fly in predatory circles above where Mira's house sits across The Divide. I never understood the human act of holding hands, not until last night. That simple touch of flesh was exhilarating, calming, and yet somehow extremely erotic. She wasn't afraid of my claws. In fact, she didn't seem scared at all.

I, on the other hand, was terrified. Terrified that another monster would slip through my awareness and seize the opportunity to pull her from her home. And I was just as scared that she would pull away and leave me bereft without her touch. Yet despite all that, I was at ease sitting there talking with her. Even with my wings scrunched and my legs unable to stretch out, I was content. I was happy.

Now, there are just a few more moments until The Divide falls. This stretch of time without her seemed much longer than the last. Still, I distracted myself by finding a way to secure the present she gave me for all to see. And then I hunted. And after the hunt, after the rush, the chase, the blood, the screams ... I showered and forced myself to rest. I wanted to be fresh and at my best for my sweet desire.

As soon as the final warning siren shrieks through from her realm to mine, The Divide falls and I dive towards her house. Her front door is already open, and she strains her gaze towards the sky, almost to the point of tumbling over her threshold. I land with more force than I intended, but the thought of her outside her protections sends a visceral fear through me that I can't control. She yelps at my sudden appearance, her mouth falling open, and my gaze lands on her lips. I want to taste her kiss again. My entire body yearns for her. But then her eyes flick to my horns, and her eyes go wide. "Is that ...?"

Lifting my arm, I flick the little dagger and wing charm that's attached to the middle of my left horn by a silver cuff. "I wear my present from my ma—Mira proudly." I watch her face to see if she caught my near slip. I don't think she's ready to know she's my mate. But my mouth, my body, my heart, wants her to know, to accept, to love me back.

She twines her fingers in front of her. "Paine, you don't have to wear it. It wasn't a—"

Holding up a hand, I halt her words. "I wear it with pride." I give my head a little shake, and the charm clinks against my horn. "I enjoy the sound it makes when I move. If my thoughts ever stray from you, the sound of your gift will bring my mind back to my sweet desire."

She sighs with a shake of her head, but there's a light in her eyes that tells me she's pleased as she says, "You are just too much sometimes."

I cock my head. "But, you like it?"

She smiles, and my heart stops before galloping ahead as she nods. "Yes. I like it."

I bow, tipping my horns to her in a show of respect that I know she doesn't understand, but I give to her all the same. As I stand, I shift and my thigh bumps into something. Looking down, I notice a padded stool. My eyes lift to her face, and her cheeks turn a pretty pink. She takes a seat on a chair that wasn't in her hall yesterday and sweeps her arm towards the stool on my side of the threshold as she explains. "It didn't look all that comfortable for you last night ... with your wings, so I thought ... I mean, if you want to stay again. I don't mean to presume ..."

Flaring my wings out, I sit. The little bench is comfortable, and the lack of back allows me to let my wings hang naturally. I bow to her again. "It means the world to me that you considered my comfort. And of course I want to stay." Her fingers curl and uncurl in her lap as if she's searching for something to say, so I settle more deeply into the soft cushion of the stool and ask, "So, what should we discuss tonight?"

With a little sigh, she shimmies back into her chair, pulling her knees up to her chest. Then she draws a thick blanket around her, and we talk. Our conversation goes on for hours as we cover every topic that comes to mind. I can't help the pleased flush that heats my face when she admits blue is her favorite color. Her laughter fills the night when I tell her I not only hate eggnog, but don't understand what it's supposed to be. As her giggles trail off, she promises to make me eggnog cookies that she swears will win me over. And to be honest, if she handed me a full glass of the weird, thick drink right now, I'd swallow it down without complaint if it would make her happy.

We share our hopes, frustrations, goals, and desires ... though I still don't mention my biggest desire—to have her, all of her. To have my mate. To have her love.

I do my best to ignore the ticking of time, but as The Divide begins to pull at me, my muscles bunch and my shoulders tense. I hate being stolen away from her. I hate that we are forced to part. And I hate that I can't touch her without endangering her life or mine. She would either need to abandon her protective blood carvings or I would have to see if I would survive crossing into her house a second time.

I don't realize she's gone quiet until the silence presses in on my ears. I lean forward, resting my hands on my thighs. She shifts, crossing her legs under her blanket so her knees rest against the arms of her chair. Her eyes stare into mine, then my body freezes as her gaze drops to my lips. Does she think about that soft kiss on Christmas as often as I do? Mira licks her lips, and my cock jerks in my pants, a spot of precum wetting the fabric. Thankfully, I always wear dark clothing, so hopefully she won't notice. But what would her reaction be if she did?

Her face is flushed, and I'm pretty sure mine is as well. What is she thinking? Because all I can think about is pressing my lips to hers, tangling my tongue inside her mouth, biting my way down her neck. I want to hold her body against mine and grind my hard length against her soft skin so she knows exactly how she affects me.

Dropping her gaze to her lap, she fiddles her fingers together as she says with a quiet voice, "I don't mean to offend you ... I know this is a vampire thing. Well, I don't know if this is actually a vampire thing or if the lore in our stories and books is just made up, but I was wondering if, well, if I invite you in, can you cross the barrier without passing out or dying?"

I blink at her before a deadly smirk pulls at one corner of my lips. My entire body lights up at her words. She's thinking about me, about us, about touching me, and it takes every shred of strength in me to keep from growling my approval at her. Instead, I inject a teasing note into my voice. "Are you inviting me into your home, Mira?"

With her gaze still on the blanket draped around her waist, she nods. "Would that work?"

I hum, wishing to all the gods that it did work that way. She glances at me from under her lashes, and I can do no less than give her the truth. "I'm not sure. And actually, I hope not. There are monsters that have the magic of thrawl and could compel a human to invite them in."

Her gaze flicks over my shoulder as if she's convinced a monster will jump out and do just that. I chuckle, and she shivers. Does my voice please her? I want more reactions like that. I want to learn her. I want to see all of her, naked and responsive under me. My tone drops with a promise. "Don't worry, my little joy. I made my message clear, both in my realm and yours. The others know to stay away or else consider their lives forfeit."

Her breath comes quicker. "You'd kill them for coming close to me?"

She likes that idea. My sweet desire is drawn to my darkness. She is perfect. I lean dangerously close to the barrier. "I already have, my sweet desire. You saw what I did to the monsters in the street the other night. And that dremar who threatened you is no more. I tore her apart and left her for the others to feast upon her flesh."

She stares at me for a long moment, her eyes darkening, her lips parted. I'm not sure what her reaction will be, so I wait. My eyes widen as she stands, and with one sure stride, she crosses her threshold. My desire is right before me. Her small hands lift and press to my bare chest. I want to growl for her so she can hear and feel my power. So, I do. Her fingers flex against my skin. Her touch is pure sin. It sings with pleasure through my body. Without thinking, I stand and wrap my arms around her, splaying my palms across her back. Her warm sweatshirt keeps her beautiful flesh from my touch, but still, I hold her close and breathe her in. I know this is wrong. This is dangerous. She shouldn't be out here, but I find that with her in my arms, I am a weak monster. I can't let her go.

It's like a dream, one that I never want to wake from. Her hands slide up my body, reaching for my shoulders. She winces, and I cock my head at her. But then Mira pulls, and I lean down until her minty breath flutters over my face. My skin tingles and my cock aches from this beautiful agony. Her gaze holds mine for an eternity, then her lips press to mine. It's a quick kiss, barely there before it's gone, but she doesn't pull back too far. She smiles, and I remain frozen, wide eyes on her. I don't move out of fear of breaking this spell.

Reaching up, she caresses my horn, and I groan. My hips roll into hers. I know she feels my hard length, but she doesn't retreat. No, my sweet desire presses harder against me as she flicks the charm, the silver wings clinking softly as she whispers against my lips, "I really like that you're wearing it."

I press one hand to her soft cheek, my claws gently caressing her skin as my other hand encircles and lifts her wrist. I kiss her palm, and her breath hitches beautifully as I say, "And I love seeing my gift on your wrist, my little joy."

Unable to help myself, I press my lips to hers in another swift kiss, but my protective nature is riding me hard. "But you must go back across your threshold."

She moans, pressing her forehead against my chest, and I nearly toss her to the concrete of the stoop so I might lick and bite every inch of her skin. She nuzzles against me, and I hold her tighter as she says with a husky voice, "I know, but I feel safe, here in your arms, Paine. Just a little longer. Please."

And how can I deny her that, especially when I want not just a few moments, but all of them with her?

The Divide tugs at me again, the feeling like icy hands wrapping around my body, trying to yank me away, away from my mate. I grunt and take a step back, giving her the space to retreat behind her barrier. But she remains out on the stoop. Her eyes travel down my body, heat in her gaze, and she licks her lips as her eyes climb back up to my face. That look on her face, the desire, the wanting, it's almost too much.

I'm so hard it's painful, but I keep my movements slow and gentle as I close the distance between us, wrapping my arms around her to hold her against me. "I am not strong enough to force you away from me, little joy." My other hand rubs up and down her back. "I'm being pulled away, my sweet desire. Let me see that you're safe before I go."

She gives me a quick squeeze before nodding and unraveling herself from me. I take her hands as she backs up. One step. Another. Our arms stretch between us as she crosses over her threshold. I don't miss the tightening around her eyes. That's the second time she has winced with that movement. I nearly slap myself as I realize the wounds in her shoulders must be hurting her. Of course they are. I sunk my claws in deep to hold my prey still.

Damn it.

I force myself to drop her hands, and her beautiful eyes are the last thing I see before I'm ripped back to my realm of monsters and darkness.

CHAPTER 13

MIRA

The all-clear siren blares, and my body trembles with warring emotions. I fight back sudden tears. My thighs press together to try to alleviate the pulsing ache there. I'm aware of all the red flags. I see them waving right in front of me, but I ignore them.

Paine makes me feel seen and appreciated. He's a fantastic listener, and his body ... I flop into my chair as I screw my eyes shut. I can still feel every muscled inch of him pressed against me. He was so warm, so gentle. And his dick ... I thought his wingspan was impressive.

My head falls against the back of the chair as I stare at the ceiling. I need to run some errands, restock groceries, call my sister, do some laundry, run the dishwasher ... But first ...

I scramble to my feet, kicking the door closed before grabbing the banister as I climb to the second floor of my townhouse. Shoving into my bedroom, I yank open the little drawer of my nightstand, the wood scraping softly. I pull out my vibrator and flop onto my bed, slipping one hand down the front of my leggings. I'm plenty wet from that encounter with Paine, and as I slip the vibe inside, I moan, rolling my hips. Pressing the button once, I activate the vibration, then press it again to activate the added suction. My other hand snakes under my sweatshirt to cup my breast. I move the vibe in steady thrusts as I pinch my nipple. My back arches as I call out Paine's name, my toes curling. Fuck. I'm so close already.

My mind supplies me with images of him hovering over me, his grey-blue skin blocking out everything else, his wings spread wide. I imagine him kissing his way down my neck before taking one of my nipples into his mouth and biting me. Panting, I dig my heels into the mattress. I position the little suction hole of my vibe over my clit, imagining it's Paine's mouth on me.

I explode, my pussy throbbing to the beat of my racing heart. Pleasure snaps from my core up through my chest until it feels like my hair is standing on end. I contract around my vibe, milking my orgasm, my nails digging into my nipple to the point of pain. I pinch harder, imagining it's Paine's claws digging into my tender flesh, and another sharp orgasm tears through me.

As my muscles relax, I'm quick to turn off the vibrator, the buzzing and sucking now too much for my sensitive pussy. I moan as I pull it out and roll off my bed. The soft pad of my feet on the worn wood floor is the only sound in the room as I make my way to my bathroom. I somehow feel both loose and relaxed but still wound tight. I can't help but think that sex with Paine will be much better than what my vibe can give me.

I pause as I run my toy under the sink with soapy hands. Sex with Paine *will* be ... I just said, *will* be. My pussy clenches—it seems she has made up her mind, and I'm inclined to agree. But still, he's a monster.

But Paine is my monster, and I ... I trust him. I recall when he told me about killing that other dremar, and my pussy clenches again. I scowl at my reflection as I set my vibe aside to dry. "Calm down, Mira. Murder isn't a turn-on." I smile in the mirror. "Okay, it kinda is ..."

I splash some water on my face, but neither my words nor the water do anything to slow my racing heart. Forcing myself to focus on the day ahead, I put on my sherpa-lined boots, grab my keys, and head downstairs. As I step outside, I start to close the door, but pause. I glare down at the blood carvings, and questions start to bubble up in the back of my mind. Yanking the door closed, I lock it and skip down the steps. I'll do my errands, then when I get home, I'll scour the internet. There must be something somewhere about how the symbols work, and if I can temporarily break the barrier ... just long enough to allow Paine into my house ...

My thoughts drift ... of him in my kitchen leaning against the counter. Of him lounging by the fire, the warm light highlighting every muscle. Of him stalking me up the stairs, pushing me through the door, throwing me onto my bed ...

A loud clang rings out as pain snaps across my shoulder, making my injuries throb. I giggle as I realize I ran into a street light post. I try my best to remain focused and go about my day, managing to only think about Paine once or twice an hour. Mostly.

Back home, chores done, I toss in my bed, trying to nap since I didn't sleep last night. I won't be sleeping tonight, not as long as Paine is here.

I must have dozed off, because I'm jerked awake by the first curfew siren. Excitement zips through me as I leap out of bed and run a brush through my wavy hair. Anticipation has me smiling wide as I brush my teeth, then I change out of my rumpled sweatshirt and into a clean one. This sweatshirt is extra fuzzy on the inside and has a small dragon in flight over the right breast. I wonder if it'll make Paine smile.

I wiggle my toes as I slip on my fuzzy socks. I nearly slip down the stairs as I race to the first floor and fling the door open. I lean as far as I can without crossing the threshold. With my eyes on the sky and my fingers clutching the door frame, I wait.

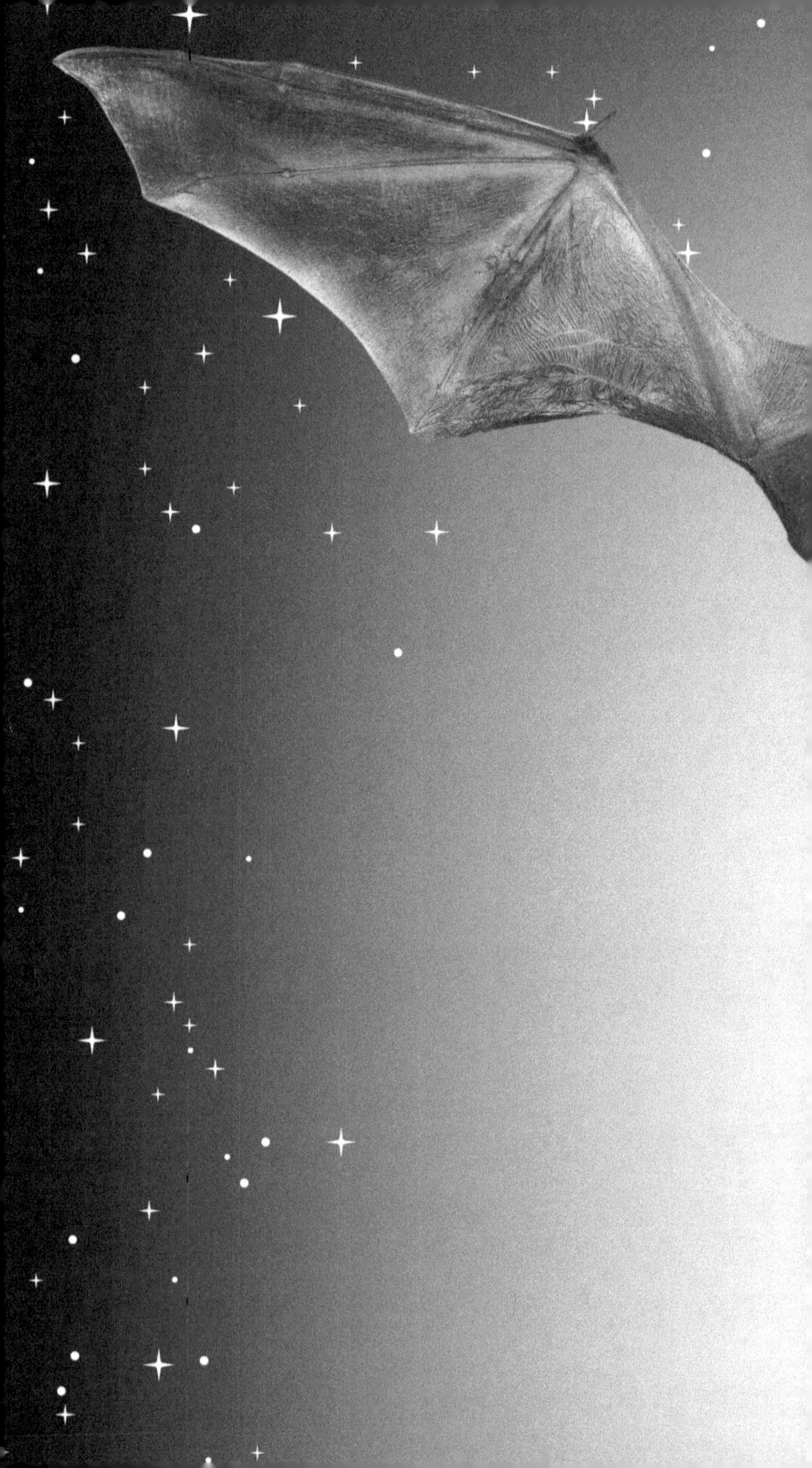

CHAPTER 14

PAINE

I'm late.

The Divide fell over four hours ago. As I pump my wings harder in pursuit of the monster I'm chasing, I wonder if Mira is looking into the sky, waiting. But this can't be helped. I've failed her too many times already. I will do this for her.

The anza on the ground blurs with another burst of its incredible speed. Damn it. The shimmer of the anza's skin glimmers in the starlight as it zigzags, trying to avoid my claws.

Flexing my fingers, I grimace at the waxy sap of the pillitar tree that coats every inch of my exposed skin. I'm panting, my wings burning with the effort just to keep up with the smaller monster on the ground, but I don't slow. With a roar and a burst of magic, I dive and manage to sink my claws into the anza's back. It screeches as I haul it off the ground, its skin going slick as it releases its hallucinogenic secretions. The sap protects me as I struggle against its thrashing. I'd forgotten how strong the anzas can be.

It tries to turn its head. One look into this creature's eyes could hypnotize me to do its bidding, but I know better. With a growl, I grab the back of its neck, my fingers easily wrapping all the way around. "Be still. I'm not after your death this turn. I need your healing ability."

The anza freezes, its throat bobbing under my fingers as it swallows. "If I heal you, you will let me go?"

"It's not me you will be healing. And if I am pleased with your efforts, yes, I will release you."

It tenses under my grip. "You want me to heal another monster?"

"No."

Like flying through an icy waterfall, I pull us both across The Divide. The anza starts to struggle again, but its movements are cut off as I squeeze its throat. Its voice is quiet but filled with disgust. "I don't like the human realm. It's too noisy, too smelly. The electricity hurts my head."

"Well, deal with it."

I drop to Mira's stoop. Her front door is open, and I'm relieved and pleased beyond measure when I see her curled up in her chair in her hallway. There's a blanket pulled up to her chin, and her eyes are closed, her lips slightly parted in sleep. I'm lost to her beauty until the anza hisses. "You want me to heal this *human*?"

With my hand still around its neck, I turn it to face me. Keeping my eyes away from theirs, I bow over it and snarl. "Yes." I lick its blood from my claws. The anza gulps, its body trembling with fear. It knows. I own it now. But just to be sure, I raise the temperature of its blood just slightly as I say, "Don't even think of trying anything." I lick the last of its blood from my skin and smile with cruel intent. "She is mine."

It trembles, and it tries to nod, but I'm holding it too tightly, so the anza croaks out, "Understood."

Releasing my magic from its blood, I spin the anza back around, and that's when I notice my little joy blinking her eyes open. When she sees me, her face lights up. My entire body tingles and feels lighter just from that one look. She's happy to see me.

I bow my head, keeping my eyes on hers. "I'm sorry I am late to return to you, my sweet desire." Holding the anza before me, I grip its neck tightly. "But this one gave me quite the chase."

Her eyes dart between the smaller monster and my face. "You ... you brought another monster to my house?"

My gaze lands on her shoulders, bringing a fresh wave of anger and guilt to the surface. I swallow, lifting my eyes back to her face. "Yes, my little joy, because this one can heal you. I'm just sorry it took me so long to properly see to your care."

She rolls her shoulders. I can tell she tries to hide the wince of pain, but I catch it, making me even more enraged at myself. As she stands, the blanket falls away. She rubs her hands down the stretchy fabric encasing her legs as she eyes the anza in my grip as she says, "It's not a big deal. I'm okay. It doesn't hurt that bad. I took some aspirin, so—"

"It's not okay, sweet desire. But this will fix it."

Mira picks at her leggings. "So, it can heal?" Her eyes go round before she leans down, trying to make eye contact with the anza. A low growl threatens to escape my throat, but I hold it in as she says, "I'm so sorry. That was incredibly rude. What is your name? Or, oh, I'm sorry if that is rude as well. I know some ... creatures don't give out their names. I, well, um ..."

I almost laugh. My sweet desire is not only apologizing to an anza, but she's worrying about its feelings? The monster in my grip looks at my mate, and I'm about to tell Mira to avoid eye contact, but it speaks with a soft voice.

"It's quite alright. I *am* a monster. I don't expect consideration from humans or monsters." Mira frowns, and the anza bows its head as much as my hold on it will allow. Its voice drops to a wistful whisper. "I am Vex."

Mira's face brightens with her beautiful smile, and I almost snap the anza's neck for it. *I* want her smiles. All of them. But I think if I kill this anza, she will be displeased with me. Besides, I still need it to heal her.

The anza continues, "While I am loath to even be in this realm, I will fulfill this dremar's request. Please, step across your barrier. This won't take long."

Mira clutches her hands and looks at me. I nod. "I've got it."

The anza chirps with a sound of derision. It seems my mate's graciousness has given it some courage as it says to me, "I am they, not *it*." The anza turns their attention back to Mira, and they lower their voice once more. "But, yes, I am well restrained. Regardless, you need not fear me. You showed me kindness, something I have never received. In return, I am happy to heal you, human."

My brows furrow as I stare at the top of the anza's small head. This creature wants to repay her kindness. Our world is all harsh violence. There's no room for patience, sympathy, or tenderness. You show kindness, you die. But my little joy has extended the simplest of courtesies to Vex and quickly earned their gratitude.

With a wary smile filled with uncertainty, Mira takes

one step across her threshold. She tugs the oversized sweatshirt over one of her shoulders, and I can't keep the growl from rumbling up my chest. Her flesh is bruised, and even though thick bandages cover the claw marks, little spots of blood have bled through.

When Vex reaches for her, I shake them so hard, their teeth rattle as I say, "Slowly."

Mira's eyes snap to mine, and there's a flash of anger there. I take the visual lashing because she doesn't understand. The anza's appearance is non-threatening, small and meek at least by monster standards—they are about the same size as my mate. But that's part of their deadly nature. If you let your guard down around an anza, you'll find yourself trapped in its hypnotizing gaze. You will fall into wild hallucinations while they peel your skin off in strips and eat you piece by piece. Death by anza can take days.

But Vex moves slowly and carefully as I keep a close eye on them. I watch for the telltale change of their skin from their natural glittering shimmer to the oil-slick that indicates they have activated their secretions. They lightly touch their fingertips to her exposed skin, and Mira tucks her chin, trying to see. Her eyes go wide, and I feel the magic of the anza flow from their body. When they pull away, they nod at her right shoulder. "Now that one, please."

Shifting, she pulls the fabric down her other arm, and the anza repeats the process. They then reach for her neck, but I growl again. "Not the bite. Leave it."

Dropping their hand, the anza stays still in my grip while Mira peers at me. Her cheeks flush pink, and I lick my lips, sending that blush down her neck. She responds so well to me, and my body hums with the desire to see what other reactions I can draw from her body.

With a shake of her head, she peels one of her bandages off. There are little pink marks where the deep punctures were. Removing the other bandage, she traces a finger over the healed skin, and whispers, "That's incredible." Her gaze lands on the anza. "Thank you, Vex."

They try to shift in my hold, and I get the sense that they are embarrassed. They whisper, "You are welcome, human. Now, Paine, I have done as you ask. Let me return home."

I didn't realize they knew my name, but it doesn't matter. Vex might be charmed by my little joy, but I'm not about to trust them. Turning, I walk them down the stairs and into the street. Several pine trees lay on their sides along the curbs, some with lights still strung through the branches. Just another thing I don't understand about this Christmas holiday. Why cut down a perfectly good tree to bring inside to decorate only to discard it?

Movement to my right draws my attention, and two monsters round a corner farther down the street. Their heads rotate as they search for prey. Panic surges through me, and I look over my shoulder, but Mira is back in her hallway, safe behind her blood carvings.

I smile at her with a nod, and she smiles back. My heart soars, but my attention is pulled away as Vex jerks with a whimper. "Please, let me go. I don't want to fight."

The approaching monsters pick up on the anza's fear. The monsters' gazes sharpen on Vex, and they both kick into a run towards us. I release Vex, and they stumble a step away from me. Their head snaps up, not in the direction of the newcomers, but towards the row of town-houses across the street. Vex lifts their chin slightly as if scenting something, then they blink away back to the monster realm. With the easy target gone, the monsters slide to a stop, assessing me before lowering their heads and backing away.

Good. I've spent too much time away from my mate.

I spin, and with a single flap of my wings, I'm on her stoop, a mere inch away from her barrier. "You are feeling better?"

Her voice is breathy as she nods. "Good as new." We hold each other's gaze, the tension crackling between us. Her fingers brush my bite mark. "You wouldn't let them heal this."

My mouth fills with saliva at the thought of biting her again, of tasting her, of fully claiming her. "It's my mark. One I want to make again, my sweet desire. I want every monster to know you are mine. And I want you to feel me through my bite even when I cannot be at your side."

Her lips drop open on a little gasp, and her chest rises and falls quickly. When her eyes fall to my mouth, my cock hardens, feeling as if it's trying to break free from my pants. There's heat in her gaze, and her teeth worry at her bottom lip as she says, "I ... I want to kiss you again."

CHAPTER 15

MIRA

Without a word, Paine uses his incredible speed to flash forward. I don't have time to call out to try to stop him. One moment he is standing still on my stoop, the next he's groaning as he backs away from the barrier. Tears silently stream down his face as he shakes his head. "I'm sorry. I can't."

The fact that he tried, even knowing the pain he would endure, makes my insides all mushy. I smile, letting some of my wicked intent spill through my eyes. "Well, I appreciate the effort, but I did a thing today."

He cocks his head, wiping the wetness from his face. With his attention zeroed in on me and me alone, my body responds. I know this isn't safe, but my baseline for safety shifted quite significantly on Christmas eve, so ...

Kneeling, I grab the knife from the floor where I left it hidden in the shadows. Paine growls, and when I look up, his eyes are on the blade. I grin and press the tip of the knife to the edge of my threshold. As I work the blade under the strip of wood, I say, "Don't worry. I'll be careful. I pried it up this afternoon. It took me a while"—actually, it took me hours of careful, painstaking work—"but I got it up in one piece, and I'm pleased to say it fits back nice and snuggly."

With a creaking pop, the wood threshold comes free. Holding it in my hand, I look up at Paine. I'm not sure how to read his expression, but I wave my free hand in invitation. Slowly, with his eyes on me, he takes one large step forward. I hold my breath, but there's no flinch, no shout of agony. Paine is in my house.

His deep voice snaps me from my thoughts. "We need to be sure." He steps back outside and waves at the empty strip. "Put it back, Mira."

I fumble as I re-secure my carved and blood-stained threshold. I thump it with the side of my fist, and it sinks into place. Paine nods, then kneels. He reaches for the threshold, his claws scraping against the edge before a snap of power zings out. He snatches his hand back. Standing, he nods. "I just wanted to make sure a monster wouldn't be able to pry it up." I blink, not having thought about that. He plants his hands on his hips, aiming a deadly grin at me. "Now, let me back in, my sweet desire."

With shaking fingers, I reverse the process, my breath hitching as Paine steps back into my house. As soon as the wood strip is back in place, I'm pulled up and spun so fast, it takes me a second to catch my bearings. I'm in Paine's arms, my body flush to his. The wing charm clinks against his horn as he growls, wrapping his arms around my waist, slanting his mouth over mine. His fangs brush my bottom lip as his tongue licks, seeking entrance. I moan, and he swallows it as my hands travel up his bare chest and over his shoulders.

He's so warm. My pulse is beating an erratic rhythm between my legs.

I'm kissing a monster.

And it's amazing.

I flick my tongue against his, the forked end strange but erotic as I think about it on other parts of my body. His chest vibrates against mine. He pushes me backwards, and my back hits the wall. He breaks the kiss as his hands tighten around my waist, his body grinding into me. His eyes search every inch of my face as if he's memorizing it. I do the same. We hold each other's gaze for a long moment.

The reality of what I've done tries to steal the excitement and desire thrumming through me. This was a great idea in the light of day, my pussy cheering me on as I worked the threshold free of the floor. Now ...

I push his chest, and the powerful monster before me takes a step back. That simple action is the sexiest thing he's done so far. I wrap my arms around my stomach, and a shiver steals down my spine. I just ...

Paine's hand lands on my shoulder, and I jump as I'm pulled from my thoughts. He drops his hand like he was burned, and I realize he thinks I flinched from his touch. I hug myself tighter as I say, "Sorry. I was just lost in thought there, and you startled me." Turning, I make my way to my little living room. "Let's get out of this cramped hallway. Come on."

I'm stalling, and my pussy is not pleased as it throbs with the need to be stretched and filled. I'm so wet, it's uncomfortable, but I just need a moment. The soft pad of his bare feet follows me, and I hear the scrape of his wings as he squeezes through the archway. I spin a little circle, keeping my arms wrapped around me. The fire crackles at my back as I shrug.

"It's not much, but it's home." My gaze falls to his broad body standing in the middle of the room, his toes curling in the thick rug.

I press my lips together to keep from laughing, but he notices and tilts his head with a smile of his own. "Are you laughing at me, little joy?"

I wave a hand at him. "You just, I mean, look at you! You're so big you make my small living room feel tiny. Your horns are practically scraping the ceiling."

His smile grows to a grin as he kneels. My smile falters at the sight of this monster on his knees before me. Fuck, he's gorgeous. The charm winks in the light, and his fangs flash. I can't help but recall how they felt brushing against my lips. His deep voice rumbles. "I like your home, Mira. Thank you for trusting me."

I nod, not sure what to say. After an awkward moment, I sputter, "Would you like some hot choc—"

He speaks at the same time. "May I touc—"

We both snap our mouths shut, smiling at each other. I wave at him. "Go ahead."

He bows his head, his dark horns tilting towards me. "May I touch you, my sweet desire?"

Yes!

All thoughts of hot chocolate are gone. My knees threaten to buckle, and I'm having a hard time drawing enough air into my lungs. I nod and watch as Paine's claws feather over my thighs, careful not to snag on my leggings. I'm frozen as his light touch climbs up, up, up, until his fingers wrap around my hips. His grip tightens, and I can't help the little gasp that leaves my lips. I've never had someone so incredibly focused on me before. In this moment, I feel like I am Paine's entire world. It's addicting. I feel drunk from his attention.

He takes a deep breath, his eyes climbing to my face. "You are such a gift, Mira."

There's so much emotion in his voice. Too much. There's obviously something more happening between us that he's not telling me. It's almost like ... magic. He leans forward, his grip pulling me to him. His lips press to my stomach through my sweatshirt, his claws digging into my hips. He pulls back enough to look up at me, and my core throbs at the desire hooding his eyes. His voice is so deep, it sends a shiver of pleasure straight between my thighs as he says, "I can't believe you are real."

His fingers slide to the hem of my sweatshirt. My eyes close, and my head falls back. Pleasure courses through me as his fingers caress the skin of my stomach. My muscles clench and flutter under his gentle touch, and my knees nearly give out again.

To steady myself, I reach for the closest thing ... his horns. I wrap my hands around them, and he growls. The sound startles me, and I rip my hands off him, but with a lightning quick move, he grabs my wrists and places my hands back where they were. "Touch me."

My lips fall open as I trace the curve of his horns. It feels extremely intimate, almost like I'm stroking his cock. That thought draws my attention downward. I can just barely make out the bulge of his dick tenting his pants, but it's hard to see much from this angle. And then my view is cut off completely as he slowly lifts my shirt and leans forward.

I moan to the ceiling as his lips kiss a wet line along the edge of my waistband. His forked tongue snakes out, and I buck into him. He groans, his hands sliding around me, his fingers delving into the back of my leggings to caress the top of my ass.

I'm a melted pile of goo in his arms as he kisses and

licks my stomach. Fuck. I'm about to come just from this. My hands grip his horns tighter, and his fingers sink lower. We both freeze when he notices. His head lifts, that wicked smirk on his lips turning my insides to fire.

"Are you not wearing any underwear, my sweet desire?"

I bite my lip with a shrug. "Laundry day?"

He chuckles, pressing his face back to my stomach, but lower than before, his nose nuzzling my pubic bone over my leggings. He takes a deep breath, and I squirm. Holding me still, he hums, sending shocks of pleasure straight to my pussy. His voice is straight sin as he says, "You smell so good. All it took was one taste of you, my Mira, and I knew. My body is yours. My life. My heart. My mate."

My eyes snap open, and he must feel the change in my body because he leans back with a frown on his lips. I blink down at him, trying to process his words. Quickly, he gets his feet under him and stands. He reaches for me but pauses. When I don't move, he gently cups my shoulders. "I'm sorry, my little joy. I didn't mean to speak those words, not yet. I know it's a lot for a human. You do not have the same mating rituals that we monsters do. I know this. I do not expect anything from you, Mira. Every allowed touch is a gift to me. Every caress, every kiss is a treasure."

He means it. He really believes he is mine and I am his. That we are ... what? Fated? Like in books? My brain buzzes with questions, but my pussy throbs with need. This monster wants me, *desires* me.

My monster.

I smile at him, and his shoulders relax.

I blink, and he's gone. The all-clear siren startles me, and I shout to the ceiling. "Fuck."

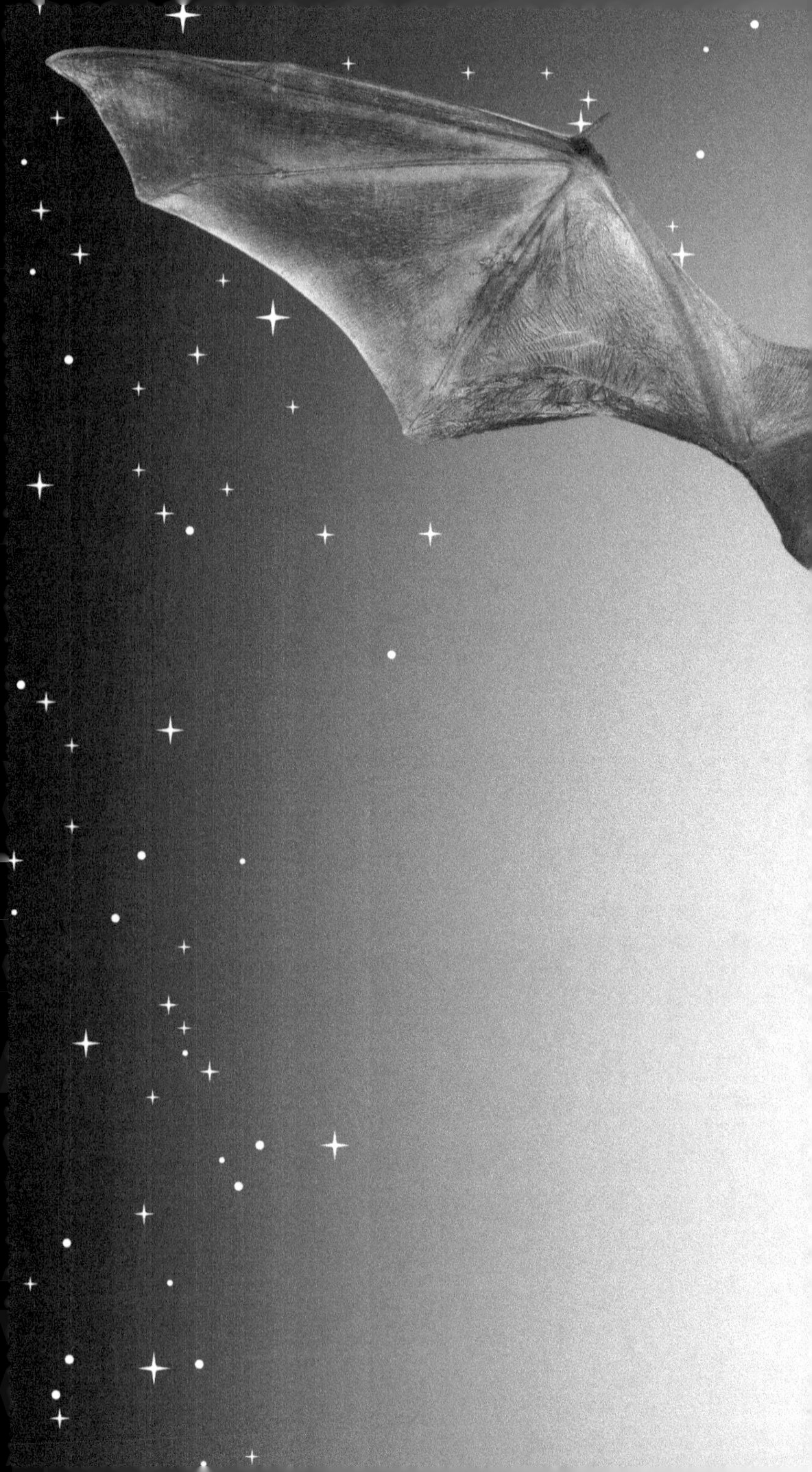

CHAPTER 16

PAINE

Fuck.

My little joy let me into her house. She was in my arms. She smiled at me after I called her my mate.

Fuck!

I don't slow as I spear towards my balcony doors, I just tuck my wings and barrel into my bedroom. With a pulse of magic, I slam the glass doors shut and shove my pants off. I grip my cock with a groan as precum coats the tip. My strokes are angry as I lament not having my sweet desire's hand around my aching length. I crave her touch, her mouth, her cunt.

Fuck!

I don't bother with any oil, using only my precum to pump my fist over my dick. It's slightly painful, but I want that bite, that edge. How dare the fates do this to me? To us?

I slow my strokes, calming as I recall her grateful

expression after the anza healed her. That alone was worth losing time with her. Her safety, her health, her comfort comes first.

Picturing her standing before me in her living room, my hand moves faster. Her skin tasted divine. I could smell her arousal, and her scent still clings to me. Dropping to my knees, I snake my thick tail between my thighs, pressing it against that sensitive spot right behind my balls. I groan, squeezing my cock as I drip onto the floor.

My stomach clenches with each stroke, my fantasies of Mira flashing behind my closed eyes. She's on her hands and knees before me, her delectable ass presented to me like the perfect Christmas present. I imagine the sounds she'd make as I scrape my claws over her ass cheeks then lower to flick her clit. She'd be dripping for me as I press my cock to her entrance. Would she want me to ease into her? Let her adjust to my size? Or would she push herself back onto me, demanding I take her like the monster I am?

With a roar, my orgasm crashes through me. I spurt cum against my stomach. My fist keeps pumping as I picture unloading into my sweet desire. My orgasm rolls and tumbles through me, shooting sparks of pleasure across every inch of my skin.

I don't bother to clean up as I just stalk to the large chair facing the windows and settle into its deep cushion. Staring into the darkness, the stars seem to mock me with their happy twinkling.

Barely an hour passes before I shove out the chair, unable to rest, unable to sit still. I yank the doors open, and with a determined flap of my wings, launch into the air. It will take me several hours to get to my destination, but it will be a good distraction as well as hopefully a productive use of my time.

The wind trails over my exposed body, and it feels good, like little tendrils of air are caressing every inch of me. It's easy to imagine my sweet desire's hands tracing over my skin, her lips, her tongue ... I nearly fall out of the sky twice as thoughts of Mira distract me. I can't help but smile as I realize what a hold she has over me. My little human has the power to command one of the most powerful dremar with nothing more than a smile and a request from her perfect lips.

The muscles of my back burn from the long flight, but I focus as the giant carved door set into the side of the mountain comes into view. If anyone knows of a way to beat The Divide, it will be the ancient one.

Now, will he agree to see me? Maybe. And if he does agree to speak with me, will he let me live for disturbing him?

I roll my shoulders, cracking my neck. I need to take the chance. I can't live being ripped away from my mate every turn. It might just drive me insane.

I rub at my aching chest.

In fact, I think it might end up killing me.

CHAPTER 17

MIRA

Staring at the sky, I nudge the threshold with my sock-covered toes. Cheers and music spill from the townhouses on either side of mine as the clocks tick over into a new year. I'm sure there's a text waiting for me from my sister and my parents, wishing me a Happy New Year, but my phone is up in my bedroom. I don't bother to retrieve it. I'll respond tomorrow. I'm in no mood to celebrate right now.

It's been two days since Paine was last here. At first, I was a ball of anticipation, waiting for him to return, hoping to finish what we started. But he didn't come.

Yesterday, when I finally fell into fitful dreams, my brain taunted me with nightmares of Paine returning only to tell me he didn't want me anymore. Or worse. The dream that woke me a few hours ago was one where he never came back. In my dream, I sat at my door night after night. I stared up at the stars, watching the other monsters roam the streets and sky, but never seeing the one I wanted. Never seeing Paine.

Yet, despite my bad dreams, here I stand, safe behind my barrier, eyes trained upwards. I wonder if I'm already living out my nightmare. Still, I wait. I hope. I want nothing more than to celebrate the New Year with my monster.

There's a flash of blue in the sky, and my heart kicks in my chest. As it circles and dives a few blocks away, I frown, noticing the wings are wrong and there's no tail on that monster. I sigh, leaning my shoulder against the door jam, my toes still poking at the threshold. Did I do something wrong? Or is he hurt?

I squeak in surprise as Paine lands with a thud on my stoop. He's breathing hard, his muscular chest heaving. There's even sweat dotting his grey-blue skin ... his exposed, naked skin. Every inch of him.

Holy shit! I know I'm staring, but I don't care. I'm so relieved, and he is ...

Paine calls my name, and I force my eyes up. He holds my gaze and opens his mouth. "I'm sorry, Mira. I did not mean to stay away. I went to see an anc—"

I drop to my knees so fast they crack against the wood floor. I don't have time to acknowledge the pain. All I care about is prying the threshold up. I grunt in frustration as the knife slips, but finally, I get the wood strip up. Waving it over my head, I grin. "Ah ha!"

With a wicked grin of his own, Paine steps into my hall. I rush to get the threshold back into place, pounding it down with my fist before standing to face my monster. His wings are tucked tightly to his back as he says, "My sweet desire. I'm so sorry. But I thin—"

Before I know what I'm doing, I leap into the air. Paine catches me, holding me against his strong body. I wrap my arms around his neck and my legs around his waist. He growls, and the little charm on his horn clinks. Pressing my lips to his neck, I kiss and lick his warm skin, and his growl deepens. With his hands on my ass, he grinds me against his cock. His tail tickles down the back seam of my leggings, and I moan, "Upstairs."

I'm lost to the sensation of Paine's body, so I'm not paying attention until my back hits my bed. His broad body takes up my entire view. He's like a looming shadow in my dark bedroom, his wings spread, his horns spiraling, his tail thrashing. Claw-tipped fingers reach for me, and every inch of my skin tingles in anticipation.

The bed dips and actually creaks under his weight as he crawls over me. He hovers close, not touching, but his heat covers me like a blanket. I can't believe this is really happening. His dark eyes travel down my body and back up again. I swallow, lifting my hips as he carefully slides two fingers under my waistband. As he peels my leggings off, the rumbling in his chest gets deeper and louder until the bed vibrates with the sound.

His gaze lands on my exposed pussy, and I fight the desire to squirm. There's a monster in my bed, and I've never been this turned on in all my thirty-eight years. His eyes find mine, and he takes a deep inhale, his broad chest expanding, his muscles flexing.

"My sweet desire."

I melt at the endearment. My skin flares hot when he grabs my inner thighs, pressing me wide. Leaning down, his wings drape over the edges of the bed as his smooth tail curls between us, tracing tortuous feather-light touches over my stomach.

My back arches, and my head presses into the mattress as Paine's forked tongue licks between my folds.

He hums in pleasure, and the sound sends my arousal even higher.

"Yes, oh yes, Paine. Do that again."

A dark chuckle rumbles against my pussy, and he begins licking and nipping. His fangs scrape my clit, and I slam my hips into his face with a moan. His claws scratch over my thigh as he releases me only to grab my wrist where my hand is bunched in the bedding. Paine places my hand on his horn, and the little wing charm clinks against my fingers.

With his mouth still on me, he looks up my body, meeting my gaze. My orgasm is building, pulsing stronger with every lick and suck of his mouth. His fingers wrap around mine, directing me to grab his horn as he says, "Hold tight, Mira."

"Fuck!"

He dives in, and I ride his face, now gripping both horns. Paine eats me with wet slurps and growling nips. It feels sinful. I'm climbing higher. My heart is racing. I'm riding a wave of pleasure, and I'm about to tumble into the crashing surf.

His tail slides under my sweatshirt, pushing it over my chest. He curls his tail around my breast, and I writhe under the overwhelming sensation that is Paine. My monster. The tip of his tail brushes over my nipple—there and gone just as quickly. I make a noise of protest, but Paine's grip on my thighs tightens, and he shoves my knees up to either side of my waist.

At this angle, his tongue thrusts deeper, his saliva dripping between my ass cheeks. His tail leaves my breast only to probe between my ass cheeks. I gasp, my muscles clenching.

"Paine!"

"Yes, my sweet desire. You are so beautiful. I could watch you unravel under me for hours. Days. Eternity."

His tail swirls in his saliva before it slips past the tight ring of my ass. His mouth closes around my clit and he sucks. My body convulses so hard, I lose my grip on his horns. Sheer bliss rips through me, filling me, shattering me. I squirt my release on his face and feel it dripping onto the bed. There's a split second of embarrassment. I've never squirted before, but Paine keeps sucking and licking. His tail pumps shallow thrusts in my ass, and I'm lost once again to pleasure as my orgasm continues to pulse through me. His growling voice seems to float all around me. "Mmm. So perfect."

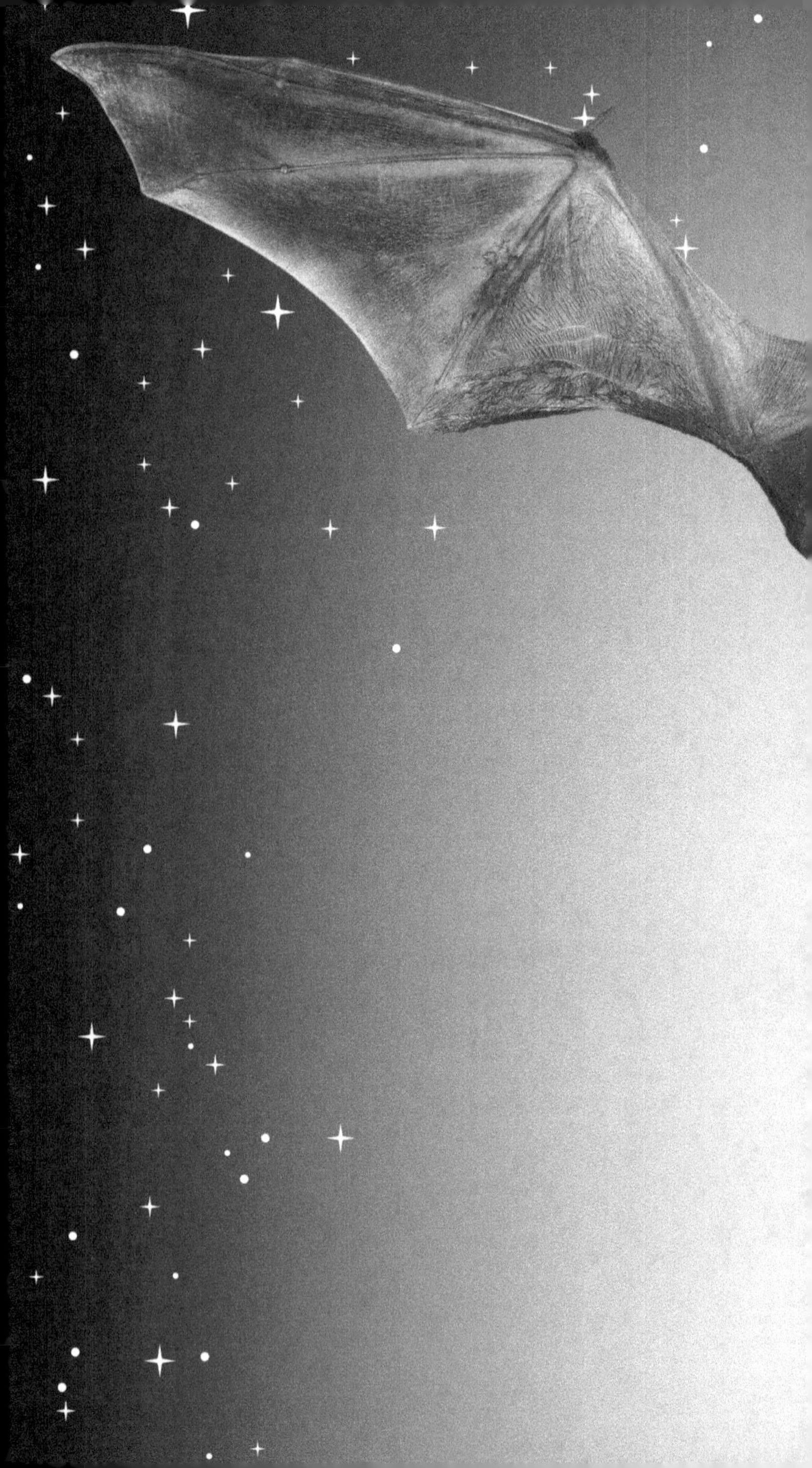

CHAPTER 18

PAINE

My sweet desire is like a drug. I'm addicted and I'll never be able to quit her.

With her taste in my mouth, and her scent all over my face, I crawl up her body, slipping my tail out of her tight ass. The tug of The Divide has been pulling at me for the past few minutes, but I needed her first orgasm before I do this.

I'm running out of time, though. I have to trust that the fates know what they are doing in pairing me with this delectable human. Dragging my leaking cock through Mira's soaked folds, I watch her with wonder as she squirms under me, obviously sensitive. Her skin is beautifully flushed, and I need to see all of her.

Running my hands under her bunched-up shirt, I wrap an arm around her waist, lifting her upper body so I can pull her sweatshirt off. It flutters to the floor, and I press a kiss to the swell of one breast as I lay her back down. She arches into me, responding perfectly.

My mate.

For a brief moment, the cloud of arousal clears from her eyes, and she bites her lip as she says, "I'm on the pill, but will that work with, well ...?"

One day, if she so desires, and if it's possible, my mate will carry our child. But until then ... I caress her skin, watching the trail of goosebumps that follow my touch. "I'm not sure, my little joy. But my seed is sterile until I want it to take root. So, until we have that discussion, until you are sure and have voiced otherwise, you have nothing to fear." Leaning down, I brush my lips over hers before whispering, "Is that okay?"

She nods eagerly, her hips lifting to rub against me, heat flaring back into her gaze. Thank fuck, because I'm about to lose all control. Dipping my head, I pull her nipple into my mouth and fist my cock, lining it up at her entrance. She grinds herself against me, and I groan, switching to her other breast. Pleasure shoots down my spine as she grabs back onto my horns, pulling my face to hers. This small human completely undoes me as she crashes her lips to mine. Our tongues dance as she tries to sink herself onto my length from her position under me.

She's so wet, so ready, so eager, but ...

The Divide pulls at me again. I'm out of time.

Lifting away from her kiss, I hold her gaze. Wonder and gratitude fill my heart as I say, "My joy, my pleasure, my desire. *Mira.*"

Her body moves under mine, the scent of her arousal filling the room. My claws look lethal against her skin as my fingers grip the underside of her chin, tilting her head back. She moans, her throat flexing. My body is lit like a live wire, my magic buzzing and pulsing inside me.

The icy grip of The Divides wraps around me, harder this time. Anger flashes through my blood. It cannot have me. Not this night or any other.

With a snap of my hips, my cock rams into my sweet desire as my teeth and fangs sink into her neck right over the bite mark I gave her on Christmas eve. Her scream of pain and pleasure rings through my ears as I drink her intoxicating blood, my thrusts hitting her deep with every stroke. My perfect mate holds me to her neck by my horns, writhing and moaning as her pussy clenches around me.

Her panting whimpers are like music. "Yes, Paine, oh, fuck. I'm going to ... I'm ... yes, oh fuck, oh fuck, oh FUUUUUCK!"

Her orgasm crashes around me, sweeping me along with her. I throw back my head, her blood coating my lips as I roar to the ceiling. The windows rattle, and several answering roars, barks, and howls come from far away. The other monsters hear me and understand my claim.

This human is my mate.

My frantic thrusts slow, and as Mira's body relaxes back into the mattress, I settle some of my weight on her, licking my bite mark. My mate mark. She turns her head to give me better access, and my heart swells with love.

So perfect, my mate.

I'm still deep inside my sweet desire as I lift my head from her neck. Keeping myself propped on one forearm, I comb the fingers of my free hand carefully through her hair, scraping her scalp. She sighs with a smile, and I make a mental note. My mate likes this touch. I search her eyes, looking for pain or regret, but all I see is satisfied female.

A siren blares, and we both freeze. I know I'm gripping her too tightly, but my body is primed with fear and adrenaline. Mira turns her head, looking towards the window. It's still dark, heavy clouds hanging low in the sky. Large snowflakes dance and swirl in the air on their journey to the ground.

My little joy ignores the beauty of the winter night outside as she reaches for the bedside table, her fingers desperately scrambling for her phone. I grab it for her, handing her the little glass device. She flips it open, and her face illuminates with the blue glow. Her eyes go wide. "The Divide is back up." She drops the phone, her eyes on mine. "But you're ... you ... how?"

My chest releases the crushing tension I'd been holding, and I sigh into my mate. "I wasn't sure if it would work."

Her hands trail light touches over my arms, moving from my shoulders to my elbows and back again. I love her touch. I love that there's absolutely no hint of fear in the air as she lies sated and warm under me.

Lightly scratching her scalp once more, I press a kiss to her lips before I explain. "That was why I was late to return to you. I went to see an ancient one. He lives several hours from me in the great mountain and is quite fickle. He kept me waiting a full turn and a half before he even agreed to see me."

"An ancient one?"

I press my lips together, trying to find the words to describe him. Finally, I just shake my head. "A tale for another day. The important thing is he did eventually hint that a true mating bond could possibly be stronger than the magic of The Divide."

Her fingers trace over my bite mark, and she shivers. "Mating bond?"

Grabbing her hand, I press it over my heart. "You are my soulmate, Mira. And I am yours. The bond you humans write of in your fictional stories is real." I lace our fingers, worried how she'll react to my claiming of her. "I should have asked first. I'm ... The Divide ... it was pulling me away ... I didn't want ... I couldn't—"

Her eyes pinch with concern, and I rush to say, "And look." My magic washes over me as the glamour I practiced while waiting on the ancient one falls over me, making me appear human. As distasteful as it is, I'll wear this facade for her.

With a flex of her muscles, she rises to one forearm, wrapping her free hand around my neck, pressing her lips to mine. Her tongue flicks at the seam of my mouth, and I open for her with a low moan. I kiss her slowly, relief liquefying my body.

She pulls away, her eyes traveling over my human face before she says, "I want you. The real you."

Fuck, my mate is *perfect*. I release my magic, and the glamour slips away. My tail curls around her thigh as my cock starts to harden inside her. Rolling, I tuck my wings, ignoring the discomfort of lying on them. It's worth it to see my desire straddling me, her wavy hair falling around her shoulders. Her skin is flushed, and her eyes drink me in—not as a human, but as me, as a monster. Her monster. She starts to move, her hips rolling, the movement so sensual, I know I'll hold and cherish this memory for the rest of my days.

Her breasts sway, and I start to reach for my little joy, but she leans forward, her hands cupping my face. Her fingers trail upwards, and she flicks the charm on my horn with a grin as she says, "Happy New Year, mate."

My arms wrap around her, tugging her chest to mine. I press a kiss to her neck, sucking at my bite mark and licking away the last of the blood from the quickly healing mark, the magic of our bond sealing it. She shivers, and I trail my lips up her jaw, over her cheek, ending at her lips. I kiss her once, twice, then hug her tight as I stare into my mate's eyes.

My voice is thick with emotion as I say, "The Happiest of New Years to you, my mate. My joy. My desire. My Mira."

THE END

The monsters of The Divide will continue with Vex the anza's story for Valentine's Day. Coming late March 2024.

ALSO BY T. B. WIESE

I genuinely hope you enjoyed this series. If you're interested, here are my other books - all adult fantasy with varying levels of spice.

Scan the code below for links to my Amazon author page where you'll find all my other books.

You'll also find a link to my website for signed paperbacks & hardcovers as well as swag.

ACKNOWLEDGMENTS

A huge thank you to my readers. Without you, this crazy dream of being an author would not be possible.

To all my beta & ARC readers, thank you! Debbie, Mackenzie, Erica, Cameron, Janene, Anna, and Kristina ... You had a big hand in making this series what it is today. Thank you so very much for taking the time to help me polish this story.

And lastly, I want to thank all my friends and family for cheering me on and being as excited about my characters as I am—I love my tribe.

ABOUT THE AUTHOR

T. B. Wiese is a military spouse, dog mom, photographer, Disney nerd, and lover of spicy fantasy. She loves animals (She grew up with dogs and working with horses, including working at the Tri-Circle D Ranch at Disney World), so don't be surprised when you find yourself reading lovable animal characters in her novels.

If you'd like to keep up to date with future releases as well as new swag and sales, sign up for her newsletter via link in code below.

SCAN THE CODE WITH YOUR CAMERA APP
FOR HER SOCIAL LINKS